"Let Go of Me,"
She Commanded,

her voice deadly quiet. Her slanted green eyes flashed a warning even he couldn't misunderstand, but he refused to let go. Placing one hand on each arm of her chair, he effectively trapped her.

As he leaned over her, the gold flecks in Blade's eyes burned into her defiant face. "No matter what you think, I only wanted to help you, and if you weren't so paranoid about accepting favors, you wouldn't be reacting like this."

"You're the one who's been accepting favors—my favors," Kyna lashed out. "I've been treated like a china doll all my life, but I'm a grown woman and I don't need someone to take care of me."

Blade made a sound deep in his throat and grasped her by both arms, pulling her out of the chair into brutal contact with his chest. "Can you protect yourself from me, from this?"

JANET JOYCE

resides in Ohio and is happily married to the man who swept her off her feet as a college coed; she admits that her own romance is what prompted her writing career. She and her family like camping and traveling, and are avid fans of college football. Ms. Joyce is an accomplished pianist, enjoys composing her own lyrics and reads voraciously.

Dear Reader:

SILHOUETTE DESIRE is an exciting new line of contemporary romances from Silhouette Books. During the past year, many Silhouette readers have written in telling us what other types of stories they'd like to read from Silhouette, and we've kept these comments and suggestions in mind in developing SILHOUETTE DESIRE.

DESIREs feature all of the elements you like to see in a romance, plus a more sensual, provocative story. So if you want to experience all the excitement, passion and joy of falling in love, then SILHOUETTE DESIRE is for you.

Karen Solem
Editor-in-Chief
Silhouette Books

JANET JOYCE
Run To Gold

Silhouette Desire
Published by Silhouette Books New York
America's Publisher of Contemporary Romance

SILHOUETTE BOOKS, a Division of Simon & Schuster, Inc.
1230 Avenue of the Americas, New York, N.Y. 10020

Copyright © 1984 by Janet Bieber and Joyce Thies

Distributed by Pocket Books

ISBN: 0-671-47383-2

First Silhouette Books printing June, 1984

10 9 8 7 6 5 4 3 2 1

America's Publisher of Contemporary Romance

Printed in the U.S.A.

Run To
Gold

1

Falling leaves drifting like multicolored feathers floated over the blacktopped bike trail along the Olentangy River. Kyna O'Brien, her slender figure dressed for warmth in a baggy blue sweatshirt and heavy navy sweat pants, ran at a leisurely pace, her jogging shoes making little sound on the hard path. She liked running in the early morning, before the trail became congested with students from the nearby university. The trail was sometimes used as a means to make contact with the opposite sex, but that wasn't Kyna's purpose, and she ignored the appreciative male looks cast in her direction.

Her waist-length shining black hair was a flowing flag that drew immediate attention. Flashing green eyes that slanted up at the corners warred with the serenity of her smooth oval face. A delicate nose and soft mouth combined to form features that were a mixture of madonna and minx. Kyna thought her figure was effectively camouflaged by her loose-fitting garment, but her long tapered legs flexed lithely with each step, and her pumping arms continually stretched the material of her sweatshirt across her high full breasts. She ran in a regular rhythm, fluid grace apparent in every long stride.

It was a brisk October morning, and the air was crisp. The fleeting white clouds, scudding overhead, forecasted the coming of winter. Kyna breathed deeply, letting the cool, damp musk of autumn fill her nostrils. It wouldn't be long before snow and cold temperatures would force her to do her running on an indoor track. For those few months, she would have to forego her enjoyment of the view of the slow-moving Olentangy and the fiery conflagration of trees along its banks that were dispensing leaves like rain.

She'd begun to slow her pace when she heard the sound of another early-bird jogger approaching behind her. As usual, her senses tuned to the sound, alert for anything suspicious that might warn her of impending danger. It made her angry that she couldn't seem to shake off such fears of attack. Ever since she had read about the recent attempted assault of a young coed along the bank of the river, Kyna had to force herself not to be suspicious of every man who ran past or showed interest in striking up a conversation.

Her breath came out in a long sigh of relief when a short, rotund man in a garish orange jogging suit labored past. Her lips quirked in a sympathetic smile. The man could hardly breathe, let alone have enough energy to be a threat to the woman he'd passed. Her eyes followed his panting progress until he turned off and began hobbling down a tree-lined residential street out of sight.

Nearing the point where she would begin the return

home, she heard someone else running up behind her. Expecting the other runner to stride by as soon as she politely moved over to the far right of the pavement, her fears renewed when she realized that whoever was following her was deliberately changing his pace to suit hers.

Nervously, she glanced covertly over her shoulder, then quickly ahead again. The advancing jogger was well over six feet tall and looked aggressively male. He had made no concessions to the cool temperature but was running in a pair of faded gray jersey shorts and a sleeveless white T-shirt. The lack of labored breathing coupled with the glimpse of a lean, powerful body warned her that she wouldn't be able to outrun him if he posed a threat. She was further alarmed when she realized her pace had slowed almost to a walk.

When she speeded up, so did he. She slowed down, and she heard his footsteps slacken in order to keep him behind her by several feet. It was time to act. As nonchalantly as possible, she searched the side of the path and finally spotted a fallen branch. She scooped it up off the ground and trotted on, trying to look casual as she stripped off dead leaves and carelessly tossed them aside. The man closed in, and her knuckles turned white on her makeshift weapon.

He was close enough for her to hear his even breathing, the sound giving no hint that he felt exhaustion or strain from running. She, on the other hand, was almost out of breath.

As swiftly as he had come up behind her, she knew he could have just as easily passed on by, and her anxiety increased. She kept a death grip on her club, frantically willing him to turn off the trail or dart quickly ahead. Her heart began pumping at an alarming rate as the tension built up inside her. Without looking, she could feel his eyes on her, sense that her figure was

11

being closely inspected, her every move perused by assessing male eyes.

With her peripheral vision, she glimpsed a flash of white, and then the man was beside her, running parallel. She was dwarfed by his height. Alarmed green eyes darted to his face and were greeted by a rising of his brow. She was too frightened to comment as frankly appreciative eyes moved down her throat and over the full curves of her breasts, which were heaving in agitation. Admiration flickered across his roguish features, glinted in his teasing brown eyes and showed in the pleased tilt of molded lips.

He was markedly handsome, but his good looks were no guarantee that he wasn't a mugger, or worse. She was very much aware that she had somehow become engaged in a silent battle of wits with an intimidating stranger. In that instant when their glances had met, she could tell that he wanted to challenge her to some private game he was playing. It wasn't fair, for she didn't know the rules, the moves or the ultimate goal he had in mind. All she knew was that she was alone and afraid.

She had to do something. With a sinking sensation, she knew that she'd been right in her assessment that he was in top physical condition. She couldn't outrun him, overpower him and was too frightened to form any words that might scare him away. She gave in to panic.

Dwarfed and vulnerable, she acted on instinct. She sidestepped and raised the stick. Her sudden halt surprised him, and he was a yard ahead of her before he realized what she had done. He stopped and turned back to face her, brushing a lock of dark blond hair away from his forehead.

"How about running together?" he asked in a deep

velvety voice that sent chilling shivers through her body.

"G—go away," she stammered, dismayed that she sounded so frightened and defenseless. Their eyes met, and she couldn't hold his gaze; instead, she concentrated on her weapon.

"You can't be afraid of *me*?" An incredulous grin slashed across his attractive features, and he took a step toward her.

"Don't come any closer, or I'll use this!" She brandished her weapon so he could see she would defend herself if necessary. His smile abruptly disappeared.

"You don't need that stick. I can take a hint." He backed away. "Some other time," he mumbled with disgust. Her green eyes shot up to his face, but he had already turned away, resuming the pace that had allowed him to overtake her so quickly. Before she could recover her poise, he was far ahead.

His parting words had sounded ominous, almost like a threat. She felt like a condemned prisoner given a temporary reprieve. Her eyes followed his rapidly departing figure. She took in the breadth of his shoulders, the tensing of his long muscular thighs and the captivating movement of taut buttocks beneath clinging jersey shorts. Under other circumstances, she might have attributed the rapid rate of her pulse to the natural effect a handsome, virile man had on a woman; instead, she knew her heart was racing in reaction to the terror that had gripped her.

Her knees were quivering, and it was several minutes before her limbs started functioning normally. She relived the entire incident in her mind, realizing how close she may have been to an assault, and her body chilled in reaction.

She took several steadying breaths, then threw the thick branch away from her into the underbrush and stood staring after it for several seconds. Calmer thoughts began to replace her terror as she analyzed the incident with sensible objectivity.

Looking back on the whole thing, she wondered if it had been merely a passing flirtation on his part. Because of her fears, she may very well have blown the man's actions way out of proportion. In her panic, she had almost smashed his head with a club.

Nevertheless, even if he hadn't intended to hurt her, his actions showed a total lack of sensitivity. He should have apologized for frightening her instead of turning away in disgust, as though she were the one who had been in the wrong.

Angered by both the man's actions and her own defensiveness, she brushed a long strand of black hair away from her flushed face and started to run. It was time to forget the unsettling incident and go home. She retraced her steps for the return, all the while thinking about the man she had just driven off. Devastating was the only word to describe him, and she knew that even if she hadn't been scared to death, she would have had difficulty dealing with a man who oozed sensuality from every pore.

The sun was steadily rising in the sky, already shining brightly above the oaks, which formed a wide canopy over the bike trail. A nipping wind was building, and judging that she had less than an hour before she was supposed to meet her business partner, Lenore Powers, for breakfast, Kyna decided to take a shortcut back to her apartment. She cut through a trampled section of red sumac and headed for the curving drive where her white-brick apartment complex occupied an entire block.

The unnerving incident had left her exhausted, and

she wished she could force her feet to move faster. Unfortunately, she felt as if her shoes were filled with lead weights, and her legs were like rubber. A long shudder of nerves prickled her spine as she heard a noise off to her right. She turned her head to the sound and saw a flash of white. A tight knot of apprehension gathered in her stomach. The stealthy movements of the man crouched behind the shrubs brought back the full force of the fear she had so recently commanded herself to forget. She glanced again, hearing the crack of dead branches as the large man in the small grove of underbrush crashed toward her.

It *was* he! The same man who had accosted her earlier. Now she knew what he had meant when he had said "some other time." That time was now! He had waited for her in a more opportune location and was prepared to drag her into the dense thicket. He was much too close! Needing no further evidence of his intent, she screamed in terror. Adrenaline pumped life-giving force through her legs, lending wings to her feet and energy to her heart, which sped like an overwound clock.

"Hey!" She heard him shout behind her, and she ran faster, crisscrossing between houses and racing down the quiet street on a direct course for the security of her apartment. She reached her building in less time than it had ever taken her to run the same distance before. Fumbling inside the small pocket at the waistband of her pants, she searched frantically for her key. Her lungs were straining for air, and she felt ill until she finally found the right one and inserted it into the large lock.

She pulled open the heavy glass door and didn't wait for the air lock to take hold but pushed back against it with all her weight, only daring to breathe again when the heavy bolt clicked into place. Safe inside the locked building, she searched the street but could see no sign of the man who had stalked her. Traffic was picking up as the residents of the complex started leaving for work, and after several fear-filled seconds of searching, Kyna decided that the man had not followed her, after all.

Limp with relief, she sagged against the glass door. It had been a close call, but she had escaped. She waited for her hammering heart to slow down, then walked shakily to the elevator which would carry her to her cozy apartment on the sixth floor.

Should she call the police and report the incident? Describe the man so they could be on the lookout for him? Had he actually done anything illegal? The answer was no, but although she was safe, she had never felt so physically spent or mentally drained.

She went methodically through the steps of removing her jogging clothes and taking a shower, hoping the warm water would relax her. She was still recovering from the incident, curled up in a chair and dressed in her robe, when there was a banging on her apartment door. The noise startled her, renewing her fright until a quick glance at her bedside clock suggested that Lenore was probably waiting outside. Kyna was supposed to have been up one floor, eating at Lenore's breakfast nook, several minutes earlier. She shook her head ruefully and went to open the door.

"Oversleep?" the sophisticated blonde woman asked, but as soon as her friend's pale features registered, she reworded her inquiry. "Aren't you feeling well?" Lenore's voice softened with concern as she searched Kyna's features for the ravaging signs of some virulent illness that might have rendered her too weak to telephone. Kyna shook her head silently, and Lenore pushed past her into the apartment. "Good

Lord! You aren't even dressed. Kyna, it's almost nine."

"I know," Kyna agreed so softly that Lenore was immediately contrite.

"Something is wrong," she intoned. "What is it? Did Mr. Lewis phone and say we didn't get the loan?" Despite her sincere concern for her friend, Lenore was a career woman from the top of her well-coiffed blonde head to the bottom of her Gucci-clad feet. The loan she and Kyna had applied for to enable them to relocate their fashionable boutique, the Gilded Lily, immediately sprang to mind. She was two years older than Kyna, but they had been fast friends since childhood. Following college, Lenore had worked as a buyer trainee for a large department store, and after Kyna's own graduation, the two women joined forces by forming their own business. Kyna's education in business and marketing was a successful addition to Lenore's natural ability in salesmanship and her training in fashion design. The Gilded Lily had shown steadily increasing profit in the last three of its four years of existence. Their hopes for more space and a better location all depended on whether or not their pro forma proved to the bank that they could repay the loan and show the developer that they would be a profitable addition to the mall.

Before Lenore could go off on a tangent for the wrong reason, Kyna guided her friend down on the flower-printed cushions of her couch. She told Lenore all that had happened on her morning jog, stressing that the man had not actually touched her or harmed her in any way but that she had felt threatened.

Talking about it with another woman who lived alone and experienced the same fears helped to ease some of Kyna's anxiety, and she was finally able to put the incident out of her mind and get ready to go to the boutique. They opened their doors at ten o'clock and had several things to do before the store was ready for its first customer. She dressed quickly in a loden-green woolen suit, pulled her hair into a tight topknot, efficiently applied her makeup and picked up her briefcase, ready for work.

"Okay, let's go." She signaled Lenore, and they left Kyna's apartment, heading for the elevator. On the ride down to the first floor, Kyna was fully occupied with finding her car keys, which always seemed to end up at the bottom of her bag. The doors slid open just as she fished out her disappearing key ring. She glanced up and stopped dead in her tracks.

"It's him!" she whispered, and bolted behind a large potted palm, dragging a startled Lenore along with her. "Lenore, that's the man!"

Kyna pointed across the lobby. A tall blond man was propped against the wall, intently studying the names above the mailboxes as if trying to locate a specific one. Was it hers? Had he somehow learned her name and tracked her to this apartment building?

"Do you think we should call the police?" Lenore whispered, eying the large, powerful stranger and trying to judge whether or not he was capable of violence.

"Hey! You there," a deep resonant voice hailed. "Could you help me?"

Lenore blurted, "Me?" tentatively reacting to the almost desperate plea in his tone.

"No!" Kyna warned adamantly, but her friend let go of her arm and stepped from behind the greenery, even though Kyna remained cringing behind the artificial palm. "Don't be foolish," Kyna tried, fear paralyzing her as she responded to the deep-timbered voice of the man she judged dangerous.

"Could you please lend me a hand?" The man took a step toward them, but then, as Kyna geared up to drag Lenore to the safety of the elevator, his right leg twisted out from beneath him, and he slowly sank to the floor. It was like watching a massive granite structure suddenly crumple to the ground before her eyes.

"He's hurt," Lenore chided, a mixture of relief and concern deepening the blue in her eyes.

Kyna lost some of her fear and stepped toward the sprawled male figure on the floor. He looked slightly dazed when he lifted his head, but then he recognized her, and an immediate change came over his features. "*You* again!" The vibrant, angry baritone made her cringe, and she wanted to step back behind the palm. Instead, she just stood there in an unmoving trance while his furious brown eyes cut into her like a blowtorch.

"Tell me, lady, do you have something against me personally, or do you refuse help to anyone in trouble?"

Lenore followed his searing gaze to Kyna's white face, then attempted to explain her friend's odd behavior toward him. "Kyna was afraid you were trying to— She thought—" She broke off with embarrassment when the man gave her an exasperated look and unsuccessfully attempted to get back to his feet.

"I don't usually conduct my conversations from the floor of a lobby. Would you mind helping me up?" he demanded, his eyes never leaving Kyna's face. "Or is that going too far out of your way?"

His wince and the suppressed oath that followed when he moved his right leg brought both women rushing to his aid. However, it was Kyna whom he chose to assist him. His long tapered fingers closed over both of her wrists as he pulled himself up with one athletic motion, balancing himself on one foot. Once standing, his hands moved up her arms and came to rest on her shoulders. Their gazes clashed, but Kyna didn't utter a sound, bracing herself to take part of his weight and at the same time willing her body not to react to the sudden oversharp tug of awareness she had felt at his first touch.

"Now what?" she asked in what she hoped was a normal tone of voice, glancing helplessly at Lenore, who stood beside them blatantly admiring his well-muscled physique.

"Hopefully nothing," he snapped, unequivocally irritated. "Nothing else could possibly go wrong this morning."

"Are you visiting someone who lives here?" Lenore asked curiously, ignoring Kyna's glare.

It was painfully obvious that Lenore found him attractive and wanted more information, but they were both late for work, and Kyna wanted out of the situation as quickly as possible. She felt an increase of pressure on her shoulders as he took a slight hop in the direction of the elevator. She turned her head and saw a gray tinge beneath the tanned skin of his face, but his tone was normal when he introduced himself.

"I'm Blade Maddox, and I'll need your help to get back to my apartment."

Kyna's stomach gave a sickening lurch as she recognized his name. "You're the new landlord?" she asked, her brows lifting in the silent hope that she was wrong.

"If you live in this building, I am," he agreed, studying her reaction to that with narrowed eyes. "And you are?"

"I'm Lenore Powers," Lenore exclaimed in an overt show of friendliness, blithely ignoring Kyna's continued glare. "And this is Kyna O'Brien. We've lived here for years and just love it, don't we, Kyna?"

"It suits our needs," Kyna offered noncommittally. He was not anything like the mental picture she had conjured up of their new landlord. The angry letter she had written to him about their recent increase in rent was sitting on her entry table, waiting to be mailed, and she was suddenly glad she had not yet sent it.

In the next second, he had draped one arm across her shoulders, and his breath teased the delicate strands of hair at the nape of her neck as he asked, "Would you mind helping me into the elevator?"

An involuntary shiver ran down her spine, and she lifted her chin to find a challenging expression in his eyes. "It shouldn't take too long," he prodded.

Giving in, she snapped impatiently, "Do you have your key?"

"I have everyone's key," he returned glibly, his sudden frank assessment of her figure throwing her completely off balance. Maybe her first impression of him had not been so far off base. He had a roguish quality that was disarming. It was difficult not to squirm beneath the increasing heaviness of the arm draped across her shoulders as he began to tell Lenore about his fall. She tried to keep her body away from the long, hard torso a hair's breadth from her side, but with every breath she drew, her breast brushed against him, and she could feel his body's warmth through the layers of her clothing. Blade Maddox was a man whom earlier that morning she had judged a mugger or worse, but now her body tightened with sensual awareness whenever he moved.

Kyna felt a surge of guilt when he told Lenore about the old football injury that had interrupted his jogging. Her cheeks went red as he explained how Kyna had run right past him without stopping to help and that he had been forced to flounder painfully back to the apartment. Although she now knew that she was perfectly safe from physical harm, she sensed that on some elemental level this particular man was a threat to her and she would be wise to have as little to do with him as possible.

"You had no intention of helping me this time, either, did you?" he inquired sarcastically while shifting his weight completely off his injured leg. He bent the limb at a slight angle until his foot was held a scant inch above the floor. When he swiveled around to keep his balance, the hair-roughened skin of his calf brushed across her legs, and she couldn't stop the wild color that flared up in her cheeks. She was sure that his move had been deliberate.

"Well, I'm glad you turned out to be harmless." Lenore saved Kyna from speaking. "Now the least we can do is get you upstairs to your apartment."

"I hope that was a compliment." He grinned and waited for Lenore to step closer. When she did, he placed an arm over her shoulder, as well, and they began to move slowly toward the elevator, with him hopping on one foot between them. After one glance at the rigid set to a very stubborn looking masculine jaw, neither the outgoing Lenore nor the outraged Kyna offered any conversation, both women keenly aware that he was concentrating on showing no sign of pain. Inside the elevator, Lenore slipped out from under his arm and went to the controls, pressing the button to close the doors.

"What floor?" she inquired, then giggled foolishly when Blade tossed her a small key. "Dumb question." She pressed the red button marked PENTHOUSE and began to chatter inanely about the building's long list of advantages. Kyna wanted to remind her of the list of complaints they had discussed the previous night but knew Lenore had forgotten every last one of them.

Blade leaned against the back wall, breathing heavily. "Damn," he muttered through tight lips as he attempted to place his foot on the floor and couldn't manage it. The oppressive weight of his arm across Kyna's shoulders became more pronounced, and she wondered if he was blaming her for his injury as well as for ignoring his cry for help. She made a move to step aside as Lenore had done, but he wouldn't release her, clamping his hand over her shoulder. Her questioning look was returned with a mocking stare, and Kyna staunchly decided it was time to take evasive action.

"I'm sorry you did this to yourself, Mr. Maddox." She tried not to flinch under the increasing pressure of a hard bicep flexed to steel. "But Lenore and I are rushed this morning. As soon as we reach your apartment, we'll have to leave you on your own."

His stare was unnerving, and she stammered. "I know this may sound stupid, but I really was afraid of you. I thought you were chasing me . . ." She trailed off before she stepped any further into the humiliating quagmire she was making for herself.

"It's true," Lenore corroborated in an abortive attempt to exonerate her friend. "Kyna was terrified when you came after her this morning. She was still shaking when I met her an hour later."

The impact of his opaque brown eyes was abrupt. Lenore withered like a dying vine and tried to shrink into the wall. She exchanged a despairing look with Kyna and waited expectantly for the elevator doors to slide open on the penthouse. Lenore was unaware of the possessively tight grip Blade had taken on Kyna's arm, but Kyna was aware of nothing else.

"We'll make sure you're all right before we go," she

placated, lifting her shoulder until he loosened his grip.

"Thank you," he said over the top of her head, and his hand slid to rest slightly above the swell of her breast. "I'm glad I was able to convince you that I'm your landlord; otherwise, I might still be sprawled on the lobby floor."

2

━━◦◦◦◦◦◦◦◦◦◦◦◦◦◦━━

I would have done the same for anyone who had taken a header onto the floor." There was a distinctive bite in Kyna's tone that seemed to make no impression on Blade, but she refused to acknowledge his disapproval. She wasn't guilty of trying to butter him up. He would know that wasn't the case when he was faced with a list of complaints about his building—that is, if she sent the letter. Besides, she thought angrily, after that morning's episode along the jogging trail, he was lucky she was willing to share the same elevator with him, let alone offer any assistance.

"I could tell," he said smoothly as the doors slid open on the plush white-carpeted entry of the penthouse. Kyna's eyes widened as her heels sank into the thick pile. She had a ridiculous, ill-timed urge to kick off her shoes and bury her toes in the exquisite rug. Instead, she and Lenore helped Blade into the large living room.

Lifting his arms from their shoulders, Blade gingerly lowered himself onto a low-slung modular section of the couch, which faced a wall of windows. Kyna's eyes unconsciously followed him down, her entirely female appreciation of the flexing masculine muscles rippling along his shoulders, his powerful thighs and muscular chest, overriding her displeasure with the man himself.

Kyna was unaware that Lenore had noticed her unusual preoccupation with a man's body. But she knew her friend was up to something when Lenore retraced her steps to the elevator and called, "Kyna, why don't you call Blade's doctor for him. I'll go open the store. See you later."

The elevator door slid closed on her smiling face before Kyna could do anything but gape. Benedict Arnold couldn't have turned traitor more swiftly. Given no choice, Kyna turned back to the man on the couch. "What would you like me to do?"

He cocked his brow at her, then concentrated on repositioning his injured leg more comfortably on the couch. He didn't look at her, but she knew without a doubt he was trying very hard not to laugh at her leading question. It was readily apparent to them both what he wanted from her.

"I need to catch my breath before I accept any more favors from you," he said with an oblique glance that couldn't conceal the humor pulling up the corners of his mouth.

Ignoring his innuendo, she stoically took a seat on the edge of a large hassock slightly across from him, wondering why she wasn't backtracking out of the suite as quickly as Lenore. She could feel his eyes on her legs, but she gamely said, "I've never been up here before."

"That's a relief," he returned strangely, and they

lapsed into an awkward silence until neither of them could stand the tension any longer and both spoke at once.

"Would you like me to call your doctor—?" she started.

"I'm sorry I frightened you this morning—"

The atmosphere lightened considerably when they both tried speaking again and their questions overlapped once more. Finally, Kyna clamped one hand over her mouth and grandly gestured for Blade to proceed first.

"I didn't mean to scare you." He smiled at her, accepting her offer to start off their conversation. "I didn't realize how I'd come across until later when I tried to get you to help me up out of the bushes and you took off like a scared rabbit."

"I have an overactive imagination," she said apologetically. "Proven, I think, by my camouflage technique downstairs."

"I didn't even know you were there," he admitted with a grin, then frowned when he shifted his knee on the couch.

"Shouldn't you contact your doctor?"

"Actually"—he shrugged his shoulders—"all that I really hurt was my pride. My knee clicked back into place in the elevator. Too late to save me from looking like a clumsy fool. The leg's sore but should be fine by tomorrow." His brown eyes feathered over her face. "I wanted to talk to you, and I knew you wouldn't come up here if I didn't remain on the injured list."

"What?" she exclaimed, shocked by his nonchalant declaration.

"I wanted to apologize in private." He gave her a winning smile. "Can't have our relationship starting off on the wrong foot."

Kyna's brows shot up. Relationship? The man was going too far. "I haven't noticed that we've started a relationship, Mr. Maddox."

"I know," Blade agreed calmly. "That's another reason I thought we should have this talk. It isn't often that my flirting with an attractive woman is mistaken for a criminal act. I must be losing my touch."

"You call following me for yards, staring at me, running beside me without saying one word, flirting?" Her astonishment showed in her eyes.

"I've been told that I have friendly eyes, a gentleman's face, and that I'm better off using the strong, silent approach."

"Who told you that, your mother?" Kyna blurted, wondering who could have given him such a ridiculous impression of himself. His eyes were far more than friendly; they were "bedroom eyes," warm and inviting. She noticed with increasing discomfort that the deep brown irises that had been flecked with gold when he was amused seemed fathomless dark pools as his gaze fixed intently on her.

His thick, slightly waving hair was dark blond, streaked with tan and highlighted with gold, almost duplicating the changeable color of his eyes. His expressions were usually those of a rogue, not a gentleman, and his physical appeal was so strong it was almost as if his body declared loud and clear, "Watch your step, girl. I'm after your body."

His burst of laughter was totally infectious, and Kyna's lips began twitching with the need to respond. "It *was* my mother, as a matter of fact. A boy should be able to trust his own mother to tell him the truth, shouldn't he?"

"It's been some time since you were a boy, Mr. Maddox," she reproved, allowing herself to give in to the natural down-to-earth side of the man.

"True, but she told me that only last week." He held her eyes with his, willing her to relax. "And please call me Blade." His eyes had taken on the color of warm brandy in a glass held up to the light. Breathless with the excitement he stimulated, she was unable to look away from his mesmerizing gaze. What she had believed was going to be an uncomfortable confrontation with a total stranger was turning out to be something entirely different.

"Why haven't I seen you around before?" he asked. "I try to jog nearly every morning, and this is the first time I've seen you out there."

"I don't run every day, and when I do, I try to go at a time when no one else is out. I enjoy the quiet of the morning and don't want to share it with anyone."

Blade frowned at her and shook his blond head. "Kyna, Kyna, haven't you any sense in that pretty head?"

"What do you mean?" she said bristling, instantly defensive, having been the recipient of that kind of question many times in the past.

"I mean that being out alone in the early morning could prove disastrous. What if I *had* been a rapist like you imagined? Do you really think that your stick would have protected you from me?"

"Well"—she squirmed uncomfortably under his dark scowl—"I could have warded off an attack, then run like crazy."

"Maybe you could have, but do you also make it a habit to cut through the underbrush on your way back?"

"Not—not usually," she stammered.

"Thank God for that, at least." He ran a hand through his hair and looked up at the ceiling for a moment before returning his brilliant gaze back on her. "I can appreciate that you enjoy the early-morning solitude, because I do, too, but will you promise me that you'll either go out when there are more people about or else take someone with you? In fact, if you want, I'll go with you. I'll promise not to talk. I'll even run a reasonable distance behind you." A slow grin spread across his face, and his eyes wandered down her body. "I'd enjoy the view."

Kyna squirmed uncomfortably under his slow scrutiny and then glared at him, but he remained unabashed by her censure. The leering grin remained slashed across his face, and gold glinted in his eyes.

Calmly placing her hands in her lap, ignoring his suggestive remarks, she stated firmly, "I resent having my rights infringed upon. Why can't women enjoy being by themselves like men can? I don't like the idea of taking along a bodyguard for protection."

"But that *is* reality." His voice was sharp and biting, in dramatic contrast to the playful tones he'd been using. "It may not be fair in your mind, but proving your independence is not worth the risk. There'll always be a few crazies around." His expression softened, and his voice lowered. "Promise me, Kyna. Promise you won't take stupid chances out there."

Again, she was mesmerized by the warmth in his eyes, this time accompanied by real-sounding concern in his low-pitched voice. "I—I'll be more careful. I really didn't think I was in any real danger."

He threw his head back and laughed uproariously. "You're priceless. Never say die. You didn't think you were in danger. That's why you threatened me with a club and sailed on by when I called out to you for help."

Annoyed, Kyna anxiously tried to leave without having to listen to more of his lecture. She'd spent too much of her life listening to unwarranted lectures on safety. She'd managed to escape from the protective cocoon her parents had forced on her, and she rebelled against any restrictions placed on her hard-won freedom. Standing up, she forced a polite smile. "Thanks for the advice, but I'd better be going now. Is there anything I can do for you before I leave?"

She surprised herself by sounding so controlled when her heart was fluttering like a Japanese fan, not in anger over his lecture but in sensual awareness of his virile appeal. Every time she looked at him, she noticed another feature of his body—each as fascinating as the next. She had to get out of there before she did something foolish. She had already satisfied herself that he was not injured seriously, since he refused her suggestion of a doctor, and she was becoming more and more uncomfortable with the direction of their conversation. She also wanted no more lectures on safety. His genuine concern for her was as upsetting as his outrageous flirting. She took a step toward the doorway and escape.

"There is one thing," Blade pounced on her polite offer, which he probably knew had only been issued as a gracious exit line. "Could you go into the bedroom and find an Ace bandage? There should be one in the top drawer of the dresser."

"Of course," Kyna quickly agreed; anything to get away from the disarming brown eyes, which made her feel foolish and too aware of the risks she had taken. Without thinking, she'd made the same mistakes real victims made. Instead of slowing down and looking at him, she should have run faster. Instead of running like a ninny through dense underbrush, she should have stayed out in the open. He'd been right to tell her that her stick would have been totally useless against him if he had wanted to attack her. His chastisement was well deserved, and she would not forget in the future. She was happy to find that her legs weren't trembling and she was able to walk normally.

"That way," he directed with a wave of his arm. The feel of his eyes following her the whole distance was discomforting, but she managed to locate his bedroom. It was turning out to be an oddly tantalizing interlude with an extremely attractive man. He implied that he would be seeing her again, and she knew for a fact that she wouldn't try fending him off with a club in the future.

His living room was decorated as a perfect foil for a handsome bachelor, but the bedroom took that role to the extreme. It was outrageous! Her eyes focused incredulously on a large, round waterbed that stood on a platform in the center of the room. Dim red lights cast a soft pink glow across the thick fur pelts that covered the bed. Her brows rose even higher when she spotted the pale satin sheets shimmering beneath the pelts, and she wondered how the man excused the blatant sensuality of the room to his unsuspecting partners. With his looks, he probably had no refusals.

Spying the wide control panel attached to the headboard, she was positive the electronic buttons did all of the things she imagined. Her discerning eye discovered the hidden speakers in the walls and the strategically placed recessed lighting. She wasn't surprised to see that the ceiling was covered with mirrored ceiling tiles. Her imagination soared when she spotted the lifelike sculpture of a nude man and woman, posed in a tight embrace, stationed in a prominent location before the wide windows.

It suddenly dawned on her that she was taking entirely too much time examining the hedonistic furnishings, so she marched to the massive oak chest that stood across the room. Unfortunately, her thoughts didn't accompany her feet but stayed centered on Blade's rumpled satin sheets. Unable to stop herself, she took another look and sucked in her breath when she saw the discarded pair of white briefs on the floor. She had no control over the image that instantly sprang to mind. She could picture Blade lying on his stomach across the sheets, his lean buttocks bared, his long muscular thighs stretched diagonally across the fur pelts. She blinked and imagined herself lying beside him, his golden brown head resting on her naked breasts. His sensual mouth—

"Having trouble?" His voice, calling to her from the living room, inserted itself into her fantasy and brought an instant reaction. She jumped almost an inch off the floor.

"Just a second," she blurted, and turned back to his bureau. She pulled out the top drawer, appalled when it slid completely out of the frame and dumped its contents onto the floor. She was on her knees like a shot, frantically piling his underwear and socks back into the drawer. Oh, Lord! What if he came in and saw her?

"I've done that myself," he admitted from his place by the door. He was leaning back against the door frame, holding his injured leg out in front of him.

"I'm so sorry," Kyna stammered as fiery heat moved up the back of her neck. The sound of his voice made her stomach bunch, and the reality of his standing inside the room of her recent fantasy was extremely disturbing. How amused he would be if he knew what she had been imagining. Why was she reacting that way? He was still a stranger, yet her body was emitting sensual signals at an ever-increasing rate. She was far too aware of him.

Lifting the drawer, she replaced it on the track inside the bureau, then slowly turned to face him and found he was watching her, his arms folded over his chest, his expression indulgent.

"The bandage," he reminded.

"Oh . . . yes." She cautiously reopened the drawer and pulled out a roll of flesh-toned elastic. "Is this it?"

He nodded and hopped over to his bed. He expertly eased himself onto the unsteady surface and propped his shoulders back against the headboard. "Can you help me wrap this thing?" He stretched his injured leg out in front of him, his movements causing the surface of the water-filled mattress to gently undulate.

She didn't want to go anywhere near him or that sacrificial platform he called a bed, but she knew it would be churlish to refuse, so she walked over to him and knelt down on the thick navy carpeting. "I won't make this worse, will I?"

"No. I want it wrapped for support so it doesn't slip out again. It's a damned nuisance, if you want to know the truth."

With a firm resolve to remain indifferent to both the man and the surroundings, she applied herself to the task, carefully lifting his knee to get the bandage under his leg. She made certain that her fingers were applied impersonally to the warm brown skin, but it did no good. She was tantalized by the feel of hard muscle. The curling crisp hair on his leg tickled her palm.

She pulled the elastic around his knee and attempted to secure it on the inside of his thigh with a pronged metal clip. When her fingers pressed down on the fastener, a muscle flinched in his leg, causing the mattress to sway in rhythmic motion. One look at his face told her that the reflex action was not caused by pain. She got back to her feet swiftly, before he was tempted to act on the desire she saw darkening his eyes.

"I should go." She jammed her fingers into her pockets but took them back out again when his eyes mocked her nervousness. Almost immediately thereafter, his expression changed, lost its blatant sensuality.

"I'm grateful for the tender loving care." He smiled and reached for her hand. His fingers locked around hers and effectively stayed her retreat. She stood stiffly, trying not to give in to the urge to throw herself into his arms and join him on the erotically moving mattress. "Stay put for a few more minutes." He was far too compelling a man, and before she knew what she was doing, she had agreed to stay a short while longer, and he released her hand.

"Anything else you need?" she asked, realizing too late what he might very well request. Hadn't she been fantasizing the same thing?

He sent out such mixed signals; one moment he was a leering wolf mouthing obvious lines and the next a concerned man cautioning her about her safety and extracting a promise from her that she would be more careful in the future. She wasn't sure if she liked him, even though she had never been more attracted to a man. Another glance around the room reminded her that the wolf was most likely the more apt description. She wondered if casual sex was something he truly enjoyed or did because it was expected of a wealthy bachelor. She was more confused by the minute. He was a paradox.

Again, he took her hand, and she looked down at his strong, blunt-tipped fingers. The back of his wide hand was hazed by curling golden hairs, and she was fascinated by the play of light upon it.

He turned her hand over in his and intently studied her palm. He traced her life line with one finger, while she desperately tried to keep herself from trembling.

"Mmmm. Kindness, warmth, a touch of temper, courage," he intoned in an outlandish Hungarian accent. "All eez there for me to see, darlink."

She burst out laughing, but the sound died in her throat when his fingers closed warmly over hers and his voice grew low and husky. "According to the Good Book, there once lived a woman who had all those traits. She had reason to be afraid, yet she soothed a stranger's injuries with a cool herbal balm. She offered him water from her well." A burning fire flickered in his ocher eyes. "Will you be the woman at the well for me?"

What kind of woman could resist a request like that? My kind, Kyna mentally decreed. Even if he sounded sincere, she wasn't having any. The man was a master of the art of seduction, but she chose to take his hypnotic words at face value. "Would you like me to get you a drink before I leave?"

"You're a hard woman, Kyna O'Brien. That line was an inspiration! Sheer genius!" He let go of her hand, feigning disgust. Immediately, she moved away. He snorted with self-condemnation. "I can tell I'll have to devote more time to your surrender." A line of displeasure creased his forehead. "You weren't put off by this den of iniquity, were you?"

"Forewarned is forearmed." She wrinkled her nose contemptuously at the bed. "You must admit that fur spreads, glowing pink lights and a round waterbed, no less, leave a woman in little doubt over what's expected to happen. I prefer a more subtle, sophisticated approach."

He swung his legs off the bed and stood up, but the graceful move was ruined when he placed his foot on the floor and swore under his breath. He grabbed for the headboard to keep his balance.

"Back to square one," he said, and took a steadying

breath, controlling his own discomfort before continuing. "This setup isn't mine. The penthouse belongs to the building's superintendent, Rod Williams. I'm staying here until my house is ready and Rod gets back from his vacation. Up until a week ago, I slept on the couch, and Rod used this room. I'm really a very nice guy, and all my friends tell me I'm extremely sophisticated and unusually subtle." He bowed his head mournfully but ruined his humble appeal by rolling his eyes toward her and smirking.

"I can tell." She giggled and gallantly offered her elbow to escort him back to the living room. "I'll make you that drink, but then I really have to go."

He shrugged and linked his arm through hers. "Would I be less than subtle if I asked you out to dinner tomorrow night?"

They walked slowly back to the living room as she thought over his invitation. The boutique didn't close until nine on Friday evenings, and by then she was usually too tired to want a night out. A good night's sleep seemed a more attractive proposition.

He was favoring his leg heavily by the time they reached the modular couch, and he quickly let go of her, gingerly lowering his body to the navy velour cushions. He pointed to the wet bar near the windows. "I know it's early, but a little vodka in the orange juice would be appreciated."

She found the juice and the liquor and mixed them in a tall glass tumbler. Did he plan to press the invitation, or didn't he? She added ice to the screwdriver and carried it over to him. He made no comment but took it from her outstretched hand, nodding his thanks. Perhaps he had forgotten his request for a date, or maybe he took her hesitation to mean she was not interested. Even though she didn't approve of his initial approach, didn't like how he had manipulated her into coming up to the penthouse, she wanted to see him again. "I'd rather go out on Saturday night, if that's all right with you."

"Already booked?" he demanded, and didn't look pleased by that prospect. A gush of pleasure swept over her. He had a knack for making her feel extremely desirable. She shook her head.

"Working late. I couldn't go until after closing, which is usually too late to enjoy a night out. I rarely get out of the store until well after ten. By Saturday, I'll have recovered from total exhaustion, and you'll have had more time to recuperate from that gimpy leg."

His grin was wide, and his eyes were flashing. "I'll dance you under the table Saturday night, and you can spend all day Sunday recuperating."

She returned the challenge. "You're speaking to the dance marathon winner of my senior class. You have my apartment number?"

He nodded. "Eight o'clock, and don't forget what I told you. No more running without friends at that time of the day."

The cautionary command evoked a stiffening in her spine, and a mutinous frown furrowed her brow. Her response was begrudging. "Okay, I'll be more careful."

He swiveled around as she made for the door. "If I'm taking out a marathon dancer, maybe I'd better wear track shoes."

Unable to resist his smile or the lilting challenge in his voice, her frown faded into a small smile. "You'd better not if you expect us to remain friends," she warned, and reached for the handle that would grant her access to the elevator.

"Don't worry, we'll stay friends." His tone was provocative, and she slipped out through the door.

3

The first thing Kyna saw when she stepped inside her apartment was the long white envelope addressed to Blade. She picked it up and slapped it lightly against her palm as she strolled absentmindedly into her living room.

"Still going to send that?"

"Oh, Lenore, you startled me." Kyna returned from her daydreaming and saw her friend seated on the couch, nonchalantly paging through a magazine. "What did you say?"

"Are you still going to send that letter to our new landlord now that you've met him?" Lenore asked, pretending to study the magazine, but her blue eyes were sparkling beneath her mascaraed lashes.

Kyna stared at the letter in her hand for a moment, then tossed it on the small writing desk in the corner. "Well, maybe I should give him a chance to justify the raise in rent. After all, I certainly misjudged him this morning. He . . . ah . . . he's not quite the ogre I thought."

"I should say not! He's gorgeous. What happened up there?" Lenore exclaimed impatiently as Kyna calmly picked up her briefcase and started for the door again.

"He's going to take me out to dinner." She twirled around to face her friend, a humorous gleam in her green eyes as she accused, "Weren't you supposed to open the store? What have you been doing all this time?"

"Not to worry." Lenore shrugged and gathered up her belongings to follow Kyna. "I called Jenny and asked her to go in early to open shop. That's why we hired her, if you remember. To take over when we are otherwise occupied. Now, I want to know all about Blade Maddox, every lurid detail."

"I should have known." Kyna laughed and lifted her briefcase. "Thanks for bringing this up for me. Come on, I'll give you all the details on the way. Jenny must be pulling her hair out by now, wondering if we're ever going to show up."

Twenty minutes later, they were on the selling floor of the Gilded Lily. Naturally, the one day they came in late, the place was filled to capacity with early shoppers, but Lenore managed to shoot a string of questions across the occupied expanse of changing rooms as they dashed between customers.

In whispered snatches, Kyna explained most of what had happened inside Blade's apartment, and Lenore immediately began listing his attributes, suggesting that Kyna would be able to elaborate after this date. Eventually, in exasperation, Kyna had to tell her to drop the subject. She insisted that it was too early to tell if anything would come of her acquaintance with Blade, but Lenore was convinced it was the start of a torrid affair, perhaps leading to something more permanent.

It was a full day, and Kyna was immersed in work during most of it, having only isolated moments to think about the morning's events. It had certainly been a day of contrasts. In between helping customers choose flattering clothes, counting receipts and dickering with wholesalers, her thoughts repeatedly returned to the seductive interlude in Blade's apartment and his parting words, "We'll stay friends." It was the soft but resolute delivery rather than the words themselves that worried Kyna. His powerful body, the husky sound of his voice and the warmth in his eyes certainly stirred responses in her, but he seemed too quick with his flirtatious lines, and she wondered if she could ever take anything he said seriously.

The loan officer from the bank called near closing time to tell them that they had been accepted for a loan but that they would have to show a signed lease before the bank would release funds. Bursting with happiness, Kyna called the agent who represented the developer of the shopping mall and arranged to meet with him the next morning. Lenore was as excited as she was, and they talked shop over dinner at their favorite neighborhood restaurant. They agreed that Kyna would visit the agent while Lenore managed the boutique, since finances were Kyna's area of expertise and she was better prepared to answer any questions the agent might pose.

On Friday afternoon, Kyna was seated in the offices of Palmer & Young Properties. George Masters, the agent, sat across an imposing executive desk, carefully studying the financial statements Kyna had presented to him. He seemed to be taking an inordinately long time to look at figures that had been in his possession for weeks, and Kyna had the distinct impression his stalling was merely a ploy to put her on the defensive. Unsure of his motives but determined not to be a victim of them, she remained calmly impassive while she waited.

"Your pro forma looks excellent, Miss O'Brien." Masters pulled on his bushy black mustache and eventually raised his gaze from the financial analysis long enough for Kyna to read the look on his face. Something was wrong. He hadn't met her eyes since she had first entered his office. His ruddy face seemed flushed as he asked, "How long did you say the Gilded Lily has been in business?" His eyes wandered down her figure, his expression blatantly appreciative of the tall, full-breasted young woman who sat with crossed ankles in the deep-cushioned tub chair opposite his desk.

Kyna's shining black hair was pulled back in a braided coil at the nape of her neck, but the severe style only emphasized the delicate, high cheekbones of her face and the exotic tilt of her green eyes. Her tailored vested suit and crisp white blouse were tasteful attire for a business meeting, but seated in the low chair, the narrow skirt crept up past her knees, and Master's higher chair gave him a good view.

"Four years. It's stated on the sheet." She didn't like his tone or his expression. "Our bank agreed to a ten-year loan, Mr. Masters. All they require is a signed lease before releasing funds. We want to start construction on the interior so we can open as soon as possible." There, that should impress him, she thought, refusing to accept the negative vibrations she was picking up from the pudgy little man across the table.

"Yes . . . well . . ." Masters looked away, leaning back in his chair to stare at a large painting of the

Palmer & Young office tower that occupied an impressive four square feet of the opposite wall.

"You see, my dear, four years may seem like a lifetime to someone your age, but in the world of retail, it's no proof of anything. We usually don't accept a tenant who can't prove that they've enjoyed an increasing profit for the last five years. One bad apple in the barrel and our center will start losing customers." His tone became increasingly patronizing. "The space you wanted is being considered by Taylor and Lawrence Jewelry. They've been in business over thirty years, you know."

Kyna hid her irritation and swallowed her disappointment. The Gilded Lily had shown a steady increase in profits, but only for the past three years. The increase had surged in the last two years, and Kyna had been confident that the developer would accept them. After all, it was an impressive record for a new business. George Masters had seemed so enthusiastic when she had first contacted him about renting space, but it was becoming more clear with each passing moment that he was either going to deny them a lease or pawn off a less attractive location.

"We do have a good space open in the corner next to Marshall's Hardware. Good merchant, Owen Marshall." Masters turned his chair away from her and waited for Kyna to do what was expected—pounce on the lesser location. When she remained silent, he frowned and swiveled back to her.

"Miss O'Brien, we never agreed to the space you have your eye on, and now that I realize you don't represent an established firm, I must tell you that we have serious doubts about renting to you and your partner." His pale blue eyes traveled down her trim skirt to her shapely long legs.

A sick revulsion came up in her throat. His meaning

was finally getting through to her. She listened to his suddenly thick voice and felt nauseous. "Perhaps something can be arranged between us. I could speak personally with Mrs. Young. We could get you a smaller space. Even that would provide better opportunity for you than that off-campus cubbyhole you presently occupy."

"Perhaps I should be the one to speak directly to Mrs. Young." Kyna pointedly pulled down the hem of her skirt and stared straight into the man's eyes. "We verbally agreed to a center mall space, Mr. Masters. I would like to speak to the head of your company myself before I consider anything else."

There was a visible change in Master's attitude, and a dull flush crept up his neck. "Won't change a thing, Miss O'Brien," he went on in a hurried nervous manner. "Of course, you're entitled to present your arguments directly to Mrs. Young, but I can interpret a financial statement as well as she can. You can't prove that your projection in sales can be met."

"Please arrange it, Mr. Masters." Kyna stood up and carefully replaced her reports in her briefcase. "I'll call Mrs. Young's office first thing on Monday morning to confirm the time of our meeting. Good day."

She turned on her heel and lifted her chin as she walked across the room to the exit. She didn't intend to let this odious man see what a hatchet job he'd just done on her and mustered every ounce of poise she possessed as she walked with a sure and regal step to the door. She felt queasy but willed her features to remain expressionless, fighting back the tears that threatened behind her eyes. All of their dreams were rapidly going up in smoke. She could almost hear her father's voice commanding, "Don't come running back to me when you fail."

She heard George Masters blustering and turned

back to him, her face twisted with contempt. "Don't you realize I could help you, girl?" Masters insisted with a leer. "All you have to do is cooperate with me, and in a few months you'll have your store just like you wanted."

"If I mention your methods of conducting business to Mrs. Young, you might find yourself out of a job sooner than that."

"I—I never said—" George Masters, furious, stood up from behind his desk, perspiration beading on his reddened face.

"Let's keep it that way, shall we?" Kyna opened the door and started to leave, then turned back, forcing a cold smile. "Thank you in advance for arranging my meeting with Mrs. Young."

Kyna left the office building, furious with George Masters and worried about the Gilded Lily's future. Their last chance was a meeting with Mrs. Young. She didn't believe that Masters would actually arrange a meeting for her, but somehow she'd manage it herself. They couldn't fail, not after coming so far. They had outgrown their present location, and the longer they stayed, the more money they'd lose. Gloomily, Kyna wondered whether Mrs. Young would find them any more reliable prospects for the prestigious mall space than Masters had? How could she tell Lenore that they might not be able to relocate as they had planned? She knew that Lenore was waiting for her back at the store so they could celebrate. She hated having to tell her that they had no reason to drink the bubbly yet, but her partner had to be apprised of the facts.

It was too late in the day to contact Mrs. Young, and Kyna knew she was going to spend a miserable weekend tormenting herself with anxiety over the negative possibilities. Remembering her date with Blade, she considered whether or not to call him and beg off. A picture of his lean body, dressed in clinging jersey shorts and a thin T-shirt, instantly came to mind, and she knew she would keep her date. An evening out with an attractive man was exactly what she needed to keep her thoughts off business for at least a few hours.

Lenore took the news as badly as Kyna had expected. "What do we do now?" she whispered across the doorway of an occupied dressing room. "Offering reduced designer labels in up-to-the-minute styles is a progressive idea, and all we get in return is a slimy proposition from the developer's agent. Palmer & Young is an international firm based here. Can't we bypass Masters and speak to a higher-up?"

"I intend to," Kyna whispered back, and crossed her fingers, hoping that she could schedule a meeting on her own. "I'll call on Monday to arrange an appointment with Mrs. Young. I'd love to tell her what kind of man Masters is. She's a woman who's been successful in business. Maybe she'll identify with us and give us a chance." Oh, please let that be true, Kyna prayed.

They exchanged more information off and on until closing, then drove back to their apartments in Kyna's car. By the time they had settled down in Kyna's apartment and rehashed every nuance of her meeting with George Masters, it was well after three A.M. Both of them were half-asleep when Lenore replaced her shoes on her feet. She scowled at the dregs of coffee left in her cup and got up from the couch. "Sometimes I wonder if it's worth it, don't you?" She stifled a gigantic yawn and stretched her arms over her head to loosen the kinks.

"Remember the old saying 'Know thyself, thy garments and thy merchant,'" Kyna offered. "What we've got to do is trust in ourselves. We sell the best,

46

we are different, and we *are* profitable. We have to show Palmer & Young what they'll be missing if they let us slip through their fingers. We may be a new business, but our customers already swear by us."

Lenore's softly feminine features turned fierce. "I'll go with you if you can get that meeting. If we're turned down, I want the pleasure of telling them what I think."

She remembered Kyna's plans and said, "I'll close up by myself tomorrow, and you can get home earlier to get ready for your date with Blade. I wish I was going out with some distracting man tomorrow night.

"I bumped into Mrs. Levine in the elevator yesterday. I don't know how she does it, but she always knows everything that goes on in our building. Anyway, she babbled on and on about Blade. He's having a big house built overlooking the Scioto River, and if you hadn't already guessed it, he's got plenty of money. Try to hang on to him, Kyna. If the Gilded Lily goes belly up, you can always opt for home and children."

"You're terrible!" Kyna shook her head in mock outrage, knowing that Lenore was half-serious but refusing to make an issue of it. "If you'd seen that bedroom in the penthouse, you'd realize that hearth and home is the farthest thing from Blade Maddox's mind. He insisted that the decor is all Rod Williams's doing, but the man looked completely at ease in those surroundings. I can just imagine what his house is going to be like. After all, he owns the building, so I'm sure all the special lighting and mirrored ceiling tiles Rod allegedly put in up there must have met with our Mr. Maddox's approval. There's probably a sunken tub big enough for two in the bathroom. I know it's the penthouse, but some of that stuff can't be standard equipment."

"If Blade Maddox turns out to be another George Masters, I'm giving up on the opposite sex."

"That'll be the day!" Kyna laughed and pointed to the door. "Now get out of here so I can get some sleep."

By seven o'clock Saturday night, Kyna was ready and waiting for Blade. He had mentioned dancing, so she wore a pale salmon dress of tissue crepe, the full, gathered skirt lined in matching silk. The deep vee neckline was bordered by an intricate design of glittering pearl-toned braid, and the sheer bodice revealed a lacy matching camisole. A tiny cameo, suspended on a delicate chain, nestled in the exposed cleavage. Her slender arms were shadowed beneath the full sheer sleeves, caught at the wrists in wide braid-trimmed cuffs and fastened by three tiny buttons. Her long legs were encased in sheer peach-toned hose; her feet, in medium-heeled patent shoes that strapped across her toes and ankles.

Kyna's black hair, secured at one side in a shimmering sweep with a jeweled comb, provided the only contrast to the pastel ensemble that would have been bland on someone without her striking coloring. On her, the designer dress was appealingly vibrant, the light color enlivened by the warm tones in her complexion, which still showed remnants of a deep summer tan.

She gave herself a final glance in the full-length mirror attached inside her closet door and smiled. This night, she was dressed to entice the male of the species, a definite contrast to the baggy clothes she'd worn on the jogging trail or the crisply tailored business suit Blade had last seen her wearing. Not bad for a lady who might soon lose her bread and butter, she thought as she left the room.

She intended to make the most of the evening,

enjoy dinner and dancing with a handsome man and forget all her troubles even if it killed her. Monday was soon enough to worry about whether or not she could get in to see Mrs. Young.

She opened a bottle of dry Spanish sherry and placed two glasses on the low coffee table in front of the couch. After plumping up the floral cushions and straightening the rust-colored accent pillows for the third time, she glared at the grandmother clock that stood near the front door. The stately walnut time-piece told her that she still had forty-five minutes to wait. Why did she always do that to herself? There she was, all dressed up and ready to go, and her escort wasn't due for almost an hour. She paced restlessly for another few minutes and jumped like a scalded cat when she heard a loud knock on her door.

Sure that it was Lenore, she ran to the door quickly, trying to imagine how best to get rid of her partner before Blade arrived. All she needed was for Lenore to march in on matchmaking detail. With an unwelcoming expression on her face, she pulled open the door.

"I love women who get ready much too early."

It was Blade! He smiled down at her approvingly. "I've been pacing upstairs for an hour and finally said, 'The hell with it. I'll pace at her apartment.'"

She was lost in his brown eyes, which flickered warmly over her. "I'm paced out," she admitted with a gulp. They stood for several seconds, Kyna grasping the door and Blade grinning in the hallway, until she realized she hadn't invited him inside. "Come in." She turned and swept her hand in an arc to show him toward the living room. "Would you like a glass of sherry?"

"Great." He spied her waiting glasses and promptly made himself at home on the couch, poured a measure of wine into each glass, then held hers out to her. Kyna sat down on the far end so she could lean back and talk to him.

Dressed in a slate-blue suit and a pearl-colored shirt accented by a striped silk tie, he looked wonderful. Wearing far more than the skimpy attire of their first meeting, he hadn't lost any of the aura of sensuality that surrounded him. If anything, his appeal was stronger and more compelling than ever. There was nowhere to look without being affected by it.

His hair, glowing with golden highlights throughout the soft brown thickness, accented his well-formed head. The style was natural and casual, but Kyna was sure the effect was achieved by a skilled and probably expensive stylist. His luxuriously thick hair lay a bit too perfect to represent the work of an ordinary barber. A heavy wave, falling rakishly across his wide brow, glowed like the light from a flickering candle, beckoning her to run her fingers through it. His eyes were more intoxicating than the wine as he gazed over the rim of his goblet at her, and his body, sheathed in the exquisitely tailored suit, issued a constant invitation. The scent of a fresh and altogether masculine cologne drifted faintly from him, and she fought the urge to lean closer and fill her nostrils with it.

She swallowed hard and took another sip of the sherry. "Where are we going?"

"I thought we'd go to the Hyatt. We can eat dinner in the Peppercorn Duck, then go dancing at Dooley's. That way we won't waste precious time driving around town. All we want will be under one roof."

"All we want?" One feathered brow arched provocatively. She knew by his nonchalant delivery of the information that he wasn't suggesting a night in one of the Hyatt's deluxe hotel rooms but couldn't resist teasing him. He had already realized that the decor in his bedroom hadn't endeared him to her, and she was curious to know if he had forgotten her reaction.

He hadn't, but responded to her query with only a sidelong glance of displeasure, as if deeply affronted that she would think he meant for them to partake of more than dinner and dancing at the hotel. "Excellent food to provide energy for the grueling pace I intend to set on the dance floor," he elaborated with emphasis on the words food and dance floor. "Have you forgotten my challenge?" He let his gaze wander down her shapely legs to the fragile shoes on her feet. "I doubt those will stand up to the wear and tear. I thought you were an experienced marathon dancer."

Looking down at her feet, she said defensively, "These are dancing shoes. What are you wearing?"

She wasn't prepared when he pulled up his pants legs and revealed high-topped black tennis shoes tied with outrageous orange laces. She sank back, giggling, into the cushions of the couch. "I don't believe it. You really did it."

By the Cheshire cat grin on his face, she knew he was enjoying her reaction to his outlandish choice of footgear, and she almost believed he intended to wear the hideous shoes for the whole night. She was greatly relieved when he set his glass down on the table and went to the door, returning with a pair of shining black leather shoes and a triumphant expression.

"Admit it, or I'll refuse to change. I was better prepared for our marathon than you."

"I'll cheerfully concede that you've won that one if you don't make me go out in public with a man wearing black sneakers with glow-in-the-dark laces." She watched him change shoes, admiring the sleek line of his spine, flexed beneath the smooth fabric of his jacket, as he bent over his knees to untie the laces. "I never know what to expect from you." The words came out before she could stop them.

"Part of my attraction—and my strategy." He completed his task and stood up, reaching for her hand to draw her up off the couch. Standing next to him, so close that she was enveloped by the tangy scent of his cologne and could feel the heat of his body, Kyna swayed toward him like a flexible aspen. His hands came down on her shoulders, and his head descended. The brush of warmth over her lips was not nearly enough to satisfy her, but when her mouth parted in soft invitation, his lips were already gone.

He pressed a friendly finger to the tip of her nose, and his grin was amused. "Patience, my charming challenger, the night is still young."

She was annoyed with herself that she'd been so affected by the brief kiss and he obviously hadn't. Her face must have reflected her thoughts, for he drew a finger across the furrow in her brows, his husky voice sealing the pledge. "We'll have plenty of time later."

Abruptly, she stepped away from him and marched the few steps to the closet, glad of the chance to turn her back on him so she could bring her reeling senses under control. After retrieving her coat, she was able to grant him a brilliant smile as she swept toward the door. Flourishing her coat like a cape, she pronounced archly, "We'll see."

4

As Blade guided Kyna through the lobby of the Hyatt Regency, she slowed their progress to admire the futuristic forty-foot-high brass chandelier that hung from the ceiling of the three-story atrium. She had not yet had the opportunity to see the Ohio Center and was impressed with Columbus's newest and largest complex. "I believe this place has been booked well into the year two thousand," Blade commented as they stood in the heart of the city's long-awaited convention center. It had been built to revitalize commerce, attract out-of-state business and stimulate tourism and by all reports was succeeding. "That speaks well for the trust the public has in the future of our city."

"If you tell me you're part owner of this building, too, I'm getting back in that European rocket you call a car," Kyna teased.

"If only that were true." Blade grasped her elbow, and they walked through the lobby.

After checking her coat, he escorted her to the hotel's specialty restaurant. Kyna appreciatively glanced over the decorous interior which was understated and modern, before concentrating on her menu. She was startled out of her concentration by the touch of Blade's fingers at her ear.

"This flower looks much better with your beautiful hair as a background." He'd removed a creamy gardenia from its crystal vase and tucked it in her hair.

Taken off guard, she couldn't hide her pleased blush and was intoxicated by the admiration she saw in his soft brown eyes.

"Makes you look like an exotic beauty from the South Seas," he further complimented with a roguish grin. "Your shining ebony hair was the first thing I noticed about you that morning I tried to get your attention. That and the gorgeous long legs you were hiding under those baggy sweat pants. I could tell by the way you were running that you have a perfect behind and incredible legs." As if to satisfy himself that he hadn't been mistaken, he peeked under the table and then quickly returned his gaze to hers, grinning wickedly. "I wasn't mistaken—at least about the legs. The rest may take a little more research."

"If I ever give you the chance!" Annoyed with his behavior, she narrowed her green eyes at him, hoping to erase the self-assured grin that seemed so much a part of his masculine features. Casting a furtive glance around the dining room, Kyna was relieved that apparently no one else had noticed his action or overheard his outrageous remarks.

"Ah, Kyna, my lovely, that's a challenge no red-blooded male could resist. You're an incredibly beautiful woman, and I'm only expressing my honest appreciation."

"Honest? Your compliments are too frequent and flowery to be believed," she declared fervently, needing to convince him that she was far too wise to succumb to his smooth charm. He'd already regaled her with a string of compliments all the way from the apartment building to the hotel. "Are you ever serious, Blade? Ever after something besides locating your next bed partner?"

"I'm perfectly serious about doing my best to impress you, but you're resisting every ploy."

She thought she had struck a nerve with her question, but he obviously hadn't wanted to give her a straight answer, his smile barely slipping.

"Save your ploys for somebody else," she snapped, even knowing they were as effective on her as on anyone else. Maybe most of what came out of his mouth was a well-rehearsed line, but she had to admit, if only to herself, he had an unfair amount of charm.

His expression changed to a mixture of curiosity and annoyance. "I've heard few complaints."

"Maybe that's because you take out the wrong kind of woman," she retorted heatedly. "If I thought all you had to offer was a good line, a fast car and tons of money, I'd tell you to get lost."

One brow rose sharply. "Is that so? And what else do you think I have to offer?"

"If I could get past the blarney, maybe I'd find out," Kyna said smoothly. "I must have believed you when you told me you were basically a nice guy, but you can still convince me otherwise."

He appeared to mull that over in his mind, evidently unsure how to respond. When, eventually, he did, Kyna sensed it was the first wholly truthful remark he'd made to her all evening. "Sometimes it's better to keep everything light. That way no one gets hurt."

"If we're never hurt, we often forget how to feel," Kyna replied softly. "I don't think I'd like that very much."

She wanted to reach out her hand to soothe the deep crease between his brows, but it swiftly disappeared as if it had never been. "Here comes our waiter. Shall we order?"

"Of course," Kyna knew the subject had been pointedly dropped, so she returned her attention to the menu and ordered the fresh duck. Blade chose shrimp tempura; both entrees reportedly were specialties of the house. Smoothing over the tension that still lingered between them, he encouraged her to take advantage of the "market bar," which held an extensive supply of salad fixings. Unfortunately, her brain was already telling her stomach to allow future space for one of the wide selection of delectable rich chocolate desserts displayed on a cart she could see from their table.

"I have a feeling I won't be able to walk when I leave here, let alone dance," she complained, while Blade showed her that he didn't suffer from the same problem. By the time the first course of their meal arrived, he had already eaten a huge spinach salad heaped with every possible accompaniment she could think of.

Judging by his trim waist and slim hips, Blade obviously had no trouble maintaining his weight, whereas Kyna found she had to watch what she ate in order to keep her slender figure. "Tell me about yourself," she insisted between bites of the savory duck and wild rice pilaf.

"Let's see." He grasped his chin and looked off into space. "Born into a wealthy family, I did all the things rich boys do. I went to private schools, drove fancy cars and met experienced women who taught me more than I should have known at that age.

"At twenty, I finished Harvard and went to work in the family business, expecting to take my place as president after I learned the ropes. I supposed it would take only about two weeks and approached my mother for my promotion after ten days. After explaining the hard facts of life to me, my mother laughed me out of her office."

He paused, surprising her by bringing up a remnant from their previous conversation. "That was one conversation I was forced to take seriously. In mom's book, I was a no-talent lay-about who had wasted a lot of her money and even more of my time by cruising through my formative years without accepting any responsibilities. At first I was shocked to my toes that the mother who'd given me everything money could buy was suddenly denying me something I not only wanted but thought I deserved. It was a painful lesson in humility—the first of many, I must confess." Blade leaned back in his chair, a reminiscent smile tugging at his mouth.

"I suddenly found, for the first time in my life, I had to prove my worth to the business and justify my existence to my own mother. Of course, that was a challenge I couldn't ignore, and she knew it; so I astonished both of us by going to work."

Kyna was all ears. His tongue-in-cheek dissertation was highly enlightening, and she prompted him to continue when he gave her a questioning glance, as if uncertain whether or not she was still interested. "Whereas nothing had been spared to provide me with the best possible formal education, my mother then provided me with the best practical education available.

"I started out in a staff position, learned everything there was to know about the properties we own, and now"—he paused to take a deep breath, then returned to the self-mocking tone he had used during most of his speech—"at the grand old age of thirty-five, I've finally earned the right to be considered for the presidency of the company."

Kyna was becoming more and more curious about his mother. She had to be a most dynamic woman if she could tell Blade he was a do-nothing lay-about and still retain his love and respect. His affectionate feelings for her came through in his discussion of her, yet she sensed he had left something out of his story, some part of his background that might explain his apparent preference for superficial relationships.

"What about your father?" she probed curiously. He hadn't mentioned anything about him, and Kyna was just as curious about the man who had sired a son like Blade. "Is he in the family business with your mother?"

Blade shook his head almost imperceptibly. "My father died when I was three. He was a dreamer who had no interest in my mother's family's firm. It was fortunate that my grandfather respected my mother's business sense, for when my father died, she needed something to perk her interest and allay her worry that we would end up penniless. Her father offered her his support and a working position in the company. But grandpa wasn't easy on her just because she was his daughter—if anything, he was probably harder. A fact she reminds me of whenever I start feeling sorry for myself.

"She remarried five years ago, and now it's time for her to get out of the harness and start enjoying life. She's fifty-five, and her husband, who became a partner after my grandfather died, is nearing retirement. The two of them deserve some fun, and I plan to see that they get it."

His concern for his mother and stepfather warmed Kyna's heart. "You like your mother's husband, don't you?" Kyna's question was more a statement of fact, which was confirmed by Blade's answer.

"Paul is a fine man and perfect for my mother. He was always hanging around when I was a boy. I think the man always loved her and was waiting for the day when it would finally dawn on her that she loved him. Mom fell in love with my dad when she was nineteen. He was a musician and probably seemed very exciting to her. I suppose it was the combination of his good looks and unconventional life that attracted her." Blade leaned back in his chair, raised his eyebrows and adopted an exaggerated British accent.

"My dear, she was from such a proper background and ran off with a piano player. Scandalous, positively scandalous!" Sobering, he elaborated. "Unfortunately, the exciting life she'd envisioned didn't come to pass. He expected her to stay at home while he went off on tours. He wanted a family and a home base. She was never cut out for that kind of life but tried valiantly until he was killed when his car went off a cliff. After mom recovered from the shock, she needed a new direction in her life. My grandfather suggested she go to work for him. She jumped at the chance to prove herself and worked her way up from the bottom of the company, exactly as she made me do."

"You sound very proud of her."

"I guess I am." He smiled as if the thought hadn't previously occurred to him. "That's about all there is to know about me; now it's your turn." He quirked one eyebrow at her, leaned forward and asked in a low voice, "Kyna O'Brien, what is your mysterious past?"

Not as open about herself as he, she waited until the waiter removed their dishes and served their after-dinner coffee before deciding how to begin. "I'm from a small town near Lake Erie. My parents own a hardware store there that my dad started all by himself not long before he and mom were married. I think mom and dad had almost given up on the idea of ever having children by the time I came along." She paused, wondering how much she should reveal. He had been very forthcoming, but then he obviously enjoyed a good relationship with his mother. She could sense his eyes on her, knew he was waiting for her to go on. Finally, she gave an offhand shrug, camouflaging the pain she still felt whenever she thought about her childhood.

"My parents were a lot older than those of my friends. I suppose that explains why they were so protective. I was given everything but independence. Every time I wanted to venture out of the pleasant world they had built for me, I had a fight on my hands. Of course they didn't want me to run off to the big city for college, preferred I go to school at the junior college in my home town so I could run home if I got into trouble. That was the first time I took a stand." She attempted a light laugh, but even to her own ears it sounded brittle.

She wanted to finish up her tale as quickly as possible, feeling it wasn't nearly as interesting as his had been. "After graduation, I was supposed to return home and work for my dad in the store, but I wanted to do something on my own. I had a degree in marketing with a minor in business and decided I'd only be allowed to use my ideas if I owned my own store." Not alluding to the horrendous rift her decision had caused between her and her father, she smiled.

"Lenore and I became partners and started the Gilded Lily."

Mention of the store brought back her anxiety about its future. What if she and Lenore didn't get the loan and the new location? What then? Her father had predicted she would fail, and Kyna sometimes felt he was hoping she would just so he could remind her that he'd always known what was best for her and always would. Thankfully, Lenore had acquired enough money to get their business on its feet that first year, but neither of them had the funds to support any expansion, and they definitely needed a more advantageous location to attract new customers.

"Something wrong?" Blade's voice was a welcome interruption in her morose thoughts, and before she knew it, she was telling him all about her dealings with Palmer & Young through their agent, George Masters.

"If only I could make them understand that our boutique is a going proposition. Columbus has come a long way, and our women are demanding better quality in clothes. Many have found that it's cheaper to buy clothes in Manhattan than it is in Columbus, Ohio!

"Columbus is moving into the future, competing with the large cities on the East and West coasts, and our women shouldn't be dressed in last year's fashions." She looked down and saw that her fingers were desperately clutching her coffee cup and knew that her cheeks were hot from the intensity of her feelings. She looked up to meet Blade's gaze and felt embarrassed for having gotten so carried away. "Sorry."

His expression was perfectly serious, and his brown eyes held hers until she glanced away. "Don't be sorry. I think you have a valid argument. New ideas do need a chance to grow. That's what makes for progress. Have you thought of bypassing that miserable excuse for an agent and talking directly to the head of the company?" Blade seemed to be inordinately angry concerning George Masters. Though Kyna appreciated his concern, she felt certain that he must realize that Masters was not the only executive in that kind of capacity that expected something in return for his services.

She explained that she had requested an appointment with the president and that Masters had supposedly agreed to make the arrangements. She went on to confess that she doubted that would happen because Masters might fear her divulging the tactics he had used with her. If that were the case, Kyna was sure the man wouldn't be in any hurry to set up a meeting between herself and the head lady at Palmer & Young.

Blade changed from a charming date to a hard-nosed businessman before her eyes and quickly proved that he was familiar with the procedures she had to go through in order to obtain space. She surmised that his investment company probably held shares in several shopping malls, and she thoroughly enjoyed talking with a man who understood her business. Most of her escorts had no interest in retail; they thought her boutique was "cute" and didn't recognize that it took intelligence and training to run such a business. She had found that she usually had to listen to her escorts' professional dreams, worries and goals without being encouraged to talk about her own.

It had always been that way with her parents. They had never credited her with any intelligence and still disliked hearing about her business. Their attitude had widened the chasm between them to such an extent that it had been months since she'd made even a token visit home.

She smiled at Blade. As she had hoped, he was not

just a shallow playboy who had no interest in a woman's ideas but was only concerned with getting her into bed. He was a complex individual, but she doubted many women bothered to cut through the surface charm to find the real man. They spent almost an hour discussing various alternatives she could try before Kyna brought an end to their business discussion.

"I'll keep you posted." She gave him a warm smile. "Let's get off this frustrating subject and try to have some fun tonight. You mentioned dancing, I believe?"

"So I did." Blade glanced at his watch, and a surprised look came over his face. "We both talk too much. If we don't hurry, Dooley's will close up before I prove that Prince Charming has nothing on me. Shine up those glass slippers, Cinderella, it's time for the ball."

Kyna felt exceedingly sorry for Cinderella after a few dances in Blade's arms. That fictional character had had to leave the ball at the stroke of midnight, but she got to dance until the wee hours with her prince. Blade was an expert dancer, moving fluidly whether the tempo was fast or slow. During the disco dances, she could admire his movement with her eyes, but it was during the slower numbers, when her body was pressed close to his, that she had to fight constantly against succumbing to his tantalizing spell. He moved his hands slowly up and down her spine until Kyna had the choice of melting into him in the middle of the dance floor or placing some distance between them. She attempted the latter, but Blade swiftly challenged her. "Does it bother you to dance this close?"

"Of course not," she lied. She certainly wasn't going to admit that the touch of his hands, the feel of her soft breasts pressed against his solid chest and the fresh, exhilarating scent of his cologne were driving her crazy. "It's just that the music has stopped." She started to move out of his arms, intending to return to their table, but he pulled her closer.

"It'll start again, and until it does, I don't need any music. Your body sings to me." His words were delivered in a husky whisper that feathered across her brow, and Kyna could only hope her reaction wasn't obvious. She was sure it was another line, yet delivered so expertly it sounded genuine. She yearned to believe him, give in to his magnetism, if only for that one night. Every part of her body responded to his, a liquid warmth spread through her limbs, and she was glad for the supporting arms around her, for she was sure that without them, she would have melted into a pool on the floor.

By the last dance, her head rested naturally on his shoulder, and his hands were locked firmly behind her waist as he guided her to the slow rhythm. She'd finally stopped resisting in favor of thoroughly enjoying the evening—later would be soon enough to display her immunity to him. The ball was over, but Kyna's version of Prince Charming escorted her home, and when she kicked off her slippers, Blade was there to massage her aching feet. Cinderella never had it so good.

Kyna leaned back on the cushions of her couch and smiled down at the gilded head bent over her outstretched feet. "That feels wonderful," she said with a sigh as Blade's fingers soothed the soreness in her arches. "No matter what it says in the fairy tale, I'd never be able to fit my swollen feet back into those shoes. If you were the prince, you'd never believe I'd been the princess at the ball."

"Sure I would," Blade avowed, and started stroking her ankles, the light touch of his fingertips no longer soothing but disturbing her senses in an entirely different way. "I'd jam your foot back into the shoe even if I had to cheat to do it."

Her nervous laugh turned into a sharp gasp as his fingers traveled up her calves and teased a light pattern on the backs of her knees. His hands slid up beneath the folds of her skirt along her thighs, then around her hips as he gently pulled her forward. Any protest was stopped by his lips as he leaned over her and took possession of her mouth.

The tip of his tongue against her lips stoked the embers that had been brought to a heated glow by the warmth of his hands on her legs, and desire burst into flame inside her. She opened to him. His tongue probed her mouth until she was on fire, intent on returning his devouring exploration on every level of sensation. He was delicious, and she drank thirstily of the taste of him. Her hands moved up his arms, across his shoulders, and finally her fingers ran through the silky hair she had so longed to touch.

She arched her body against him, and Blade came up off his knees to join her on the couch, his strong hands on her hips, guiding her until she lay beside him. She could feel the unleashed passion in his powerfully virile body as he pulled her softness to him. Flashes of pleasure fired through her when his hands molded her waist and buttocks, his thumbs tracing the line of her hips.

He lifted his lips, and her mouth shifted to the rugged line of his jaw, pressing small kisses until her lips reached his ear. One hand came up to capture her chin, and he gave a small groan as he turned her mouth back to his and took possession again while his fingers traveled down her throat and slid inside the bodice of her dress.

On one level, she knew she should stop him before things got completely out of hand, but his fingertips brushed lightly across the peaks of her breasts, and her nipples swelled, begging for more. The tiny round buttons down the front of her dress were released, and only the fragile lace of her camisole was between her aching breasts and his searching mouth. Seconds later, his tongue teased aside the lace, fully releasing her breasts, and flickered across their burgeoning peaks. He spanned one large hand across her bosom and slightly touched her taut nipples with his thumb and little finger. No man had ever done that to her before, and her gasping intake of breath was a reaction to the pleasure of it, compounded by the hypnotic brushing of his other thumb across her flat stomach while his fingers pressed into her buttocks. He pushed her nipples up gently, and his mouth claimed them each in turn.

"Blade!" she cried, part in reaction part in plea, her body shuddering in his arms.

"Mmmm?" His voice was sandpaper and satin as he breathed warmly over her fevered flesh, constantly reheating the passion, which was rapidly building to an inferno. His shirt, along with his jacket and tie, disappeared, and they were both reveling in the feel of their naked skin in intimate contact.

"We're going too fast," she moaned against his rough cheek. "I need time to think."

"I know exactly what you're thinking." His meaning was clear. Without words, her body was expressing her needs, telling him exactly what she wanted. With her last grasp at coherent thought, she denied what she wanted most. She stiffened away from him and was appalled at how painful it was to separate her brain from her body.

He sensed her withdrawal almost immediately, and she knew she was right to stop them when he showed no irritation or inclination to continue. He couldn't possibly feel the same way, not a man who made love so expertly she had been transported to heated heights at his first caress. He released her, his ragged breathing and flushed face demonstrating that he had been as aroused as she. He made no attempt to help her into her clothing, nor did he show any interest in her nakedness as he casually sat up and reached for his shirt. As soon as she had adjusted her camisole and rebuttoned her dress, she hugged a throw pillow to her chest, needing something to hide the lingering flickers of want that still raced in spurts through her body.

"What are your plans for tomorrow?" he asked in an even tone, but the question came as a blessed relief to her. He still wanted to see her even after she had defused the ultimate explosion that had been fast overtaking them.

"Nothing special." She matched his tone and waited for him to invite her to spend the day with him. It was coldly disappointing to have him shrug and stand up from the couch, casually rebuttoning his shirt, then tucking the ends into his pants.

"Try not to spend it worrying about your business," he advised with a smile, then picked up his jacket and slung it over his shoulder. He bent to retrieve his tennis shoes, then gave her a friendly pat on the top of her head before striding to the door, the bright orange laces dangling from the black canvas shoes swinging from his hand. The picture he made might have caused her to smile under other circumstances, but she was concentrating fully on calming her ragged breathing, trying to digest his sudden leave-taking.

He had patted her on the head as if she were some adoring puppy! Her frustration with his platonic gesture must have shown on her face, because he hesitated at the door with his hand on the knob, perhaps realizing that she hadn't followed him back up the road from passion to casual indifference.

"I'm going out to my mother's place tomorrow. Once in a while we like to spend a day together. I'll call you." His eyes probed her face for a smile, and she produced a weak one, but she would rather have thrown the pillow she was still clutching at his head.

"Fine," she called over her shoulder, and waved at him as he opened the door. There was a tight expression on his face as he went out, and Kyna wondered if it were from the same frustration she felt or merely displeasure that he hadn't been successful in his attempt to seduce her. She doubted he was used to being turned down.

His offer to call was pretty standard. Was his comment about seeing his mother a handy line he used to cover a brush-off, or was it a legitimate excuse for not calling her?

From what he had told her during dinner, she knew that he loved his mother. Maybe, he's a mama's boy, she thought nastily, then laughed harshly. There was nothing dependent or prissy about the man. Besides, what was she thinking? That after one date he owed his entire weekend to her? Would it have been any different if she'd invited him into her bed?

She pushed a loose strand of hair behind her ear and hugged the pillow more tightly to her breast, rocking back and forth to still the thunderous beating of her heart. Thank God things hadn't gone any further. She didn't go in for casual sex, but maybe that was all Blade had in mind.

Not wanting to think about it any longer, she picked

up their empty glasses from the coffee table and went to rinse them off in the sink. She was tired, but the unrelieved tension in her body kept her awake. She pulled open the door of her refrigerator and began to clean it. If she couldn't sleep, at least she could catch up on some of the neglected chores in her apartment.

5

Did you go on Lysol overload this weekend?" Lenore remarked as she surveyed the sparkling-clean appliances in Kyna's cheerful kitchen.

"You know I always clean when I'm worried." Kyna placed their empty coffee cups in the sink and ran water over them. "What if I call Palmer & Young today and they tell me to go pester some other developer?"

"We'll go pester some other developer." Lenore lifted her shoulders and quickly reached across the table for the last half-eaten Danish before Kyna could scrape it into the disposal and wash off the plate. "There are plenty of other shopping malls in town."

"Not where our preferred customers will have such easy access to us," Kyna disagreed, pacing the narrow space between the sink and the kitchen table. "If we move elsewhere, we'll have to attract brand-new customers, and you know how long that takes. Most of the women who now shop at our store are already familiar with what we have to offer. Several of them have told me they're glad we're moving closer to them instead of farther away. We need all the repeat business we can get."

Both women jumped when the phone in the living room began jangling. Kyna took a deep breath, then went to answer it. "I hope it's not Jenny calling in sick. I was counting on her to man the fort while you and I try to get an appointment with Palmer & Young."

Lenore followed Kyna into the living room as she picked up the phone. "Hello," Kyna said expectantly, her brows lifting in surprise when she recognized the voice on the other end of the phone.

"George Masters here, Miss O'Brien." The agent's tone was crisp and curt. "A meeting has been scheduled for you with Mrs. Young at two this afternoon. Please bring your pro forma and the bank's offer of financial support for her to study."

"A meeting with Mrs. Young?" As Kyna began frantically gesturing with her hands, her partner rushed to find a pencil and pad. While Kyna wrote down the time of her appointment, Lenore started dancing around the room, hugging herself with both arms.

Although experiencing the same kind of exhilaration, Kyna managed to maintain a cool tone as she pronounced, "We'll be there, Mr. Masters." Oddly enough, she had an urge to gush her thanks effusively to the odious man, who suddenly seemed to have been transformed into an angel of mercy, though she wondered what had brought about his change in attitude. She had almost been positive he wouldn't arrange a meeting between her and the developer.

She was prepared to hang up and join Lenore on the imaginary dance floor when George Masters cleared his throat as if he were having trouble swallowing. "I—I must apologize if I left you with the wrong impression last Friday," he said, and Kyna's brows rose even higher. "I was hoping that we could work more closely on the figures you showed me to sway Mrs. Young in your favor. That was all."

"Perhaps I misunderstood, Mr. Masters." Kyna felt she could now afford to be gracious, even knowing that only an idiot could have misinterpreted George Masters' implications at their meeting.

"Thank you," Masters said tensely, and she got the definite impression he was wiping his brow with his handkerchief. The man must have worried about his mishandling of things all weekend and had decided to clean the slate first thing Monday morning. His arranging for her to meet personally with Mrs. Young was proof in her book that he regretted his suggestive behavior.

"You have no idea how much we appreciate this, Mr. Masters," she exclaimed sincerely. "Thank you."

She was puzzled by his equally sincere disclaimer. "Don't thank me, Miss O'Brien," he said tightly, but hung up the phone before Kyna could ask him why not.

"It's all set." Kyna's smile was bemused as she clasped both hands to her bosom. "Maybe I was too hard on old George. He arranged the whole thing!"

A bit more cynical, Lenore laughed shortly. "The lecher must have realized it was a 'no go' and decided to cooperate before you complained to the boss."

"Maybe, maybe not." Kyna shrugged, then went to her desk and began gathering the papers they'd need to take with them. "Let's get to the boutique and tell Jenny. After that, we work out our plans for attack on all fronts. Mrs. Young will be so impressed with our business, she'll probably offer us two prime sites in the mall."

"Or three," Lenore agreed, ready to pin all their hopes on the woman who now controlled their immediate future. "I hope she's the grandmother type, a pioneer for woman's rights and part fairy godmother."

They were ushered into Mrs. Young's spacious office promptly at two that afternoon. The woman's secretary told them to make themselves at home at an immense walnut conference table. "Mrs. Young will be with you in a few minutes. She's been delayed by a long-distance call."

"There's no hurry," Lenore offered politely, waiting for the woman to close the office door behind her before saying, "Okay, I'm sufficiently terrified. Just look at this place!"

Kyna had to agree with Lenore's assessment of their surroundings, which was composed of two rooms, the conference room where they were seated and a large executive office. The floors were covered by plush ice-blue carpeting, the walls paneled in rich wood. Occupying the fifteenth floor of the Palmer & Young office tower, the rooms were given a light and airy feel by the floor-to-ceiling windows.

A brass-trimmed, mahogany campaign desk, which looked antique, provided the focal point of the office, but the other furnishings were equally impressive. Leather chairs and highly polished tables were highlighted by a variety of gleaming brass lamps.

Kyna's gaze was caught by one of the original oils that hung on the walls. She recognized the name of a local artist and noted that the paintings were for sale. If Mrs. Young was promoting the artist's work, perhaps she could also be persuaded to promote the Gilded Lily. It was quite out of the ordinary to find oil paintings on sale in an executive office suite, which made Kyna think the woman who occupied the rooms had to be a unique individual. She wondered what the influential people who passed through the office thought when they were confronted with "for sale" signs.

"You like them, Miss O'Brien?" The clear cultured tones were spoken by a svelte-looking woman dressed in a bone tweed blazer, pale blue blouse and dark brown woolen skirt. She looked to be in her early forties except for the completely white hair, which was cut short and worn off her face in a sophisticated upswept style. The woman was close to Kyna in height and equally as slender. Penetrating hazel-brown eyes, a straightforward expression and a generous smile combined to form a picture of mature friendliness and understated authority.

"Very much, Mrs. Young." Kyna stood up, never doubting she was facing the president of a multimillion-dollar corporation. Evidently, George Masters had described her appearance to the boss, for the woman obviously knew which of them was which. "My partner, Lenore Powers."

"Miss Powers." The woman extended her hand as she neared the table. Once the initial greetings were exchanged, Mrs. Young took her place at the head of the table, folding her hands together on the smooth surface. "Now, then, let's get down to business."

As Kyna began explaining each document she had brought with her, she felt increasingly more confident. The older woman smiled and nodded throughout. She did ask several pertinent questions for purposes of clarification but otherwise seemed willing to accept whatever Kyna said.

After Kyna had completed her presentation, Mrs. Young informed them that she would make her decision within three weeks, during which time she would make a close study of the figures. She also wanted to meet with Kyna and discuss Kyna's business philosophy. That seemed odd to Kyna, but she said nothing when the woman proceeded to quote them a reasonable base rent, a lower-than-expected percentage rent and Palmer & Young's assistance in obtaining adequate maintenance and equitable insurance if, indeed, the lease were signed.

Kyna felt confident that they would eventually come to terms and was amazed when Mrs. Young scanned a copy of their lease, then advised them to show it to their attorney before they considered signing.

Unlike Kyna, Lenore did not fully understand the fine points of the conversation but was aware they were close to striking a deal and was openly as pleased as Kyna. "You're considering us, then?" she asked tentatively.

"This looks like a viable proposal," Mrs. Young returned equably, "but I'll require a little more time to go over the figures. Miss O'Brien has stated your case most effectively. I admire people who do all their homework and come completely prepared with finance data and sound projections. It saves everyone a lot of time."

As she had been throughout the interview, Kyna was the recipient of an approving smile. She was puzzled, uncertain why all questions had been directed to her throughout the interview and why she felt she was the one who had just passed inspection. Part of the answer came with Mrs. Young's next statement.

"It seems that the two of you have formed an enviable partnership. Miss Powers handles sales and you the finances. I've found alliances work better when those involved have complementing strengths." Mrs. Young pressed a buzzer on the table. "Let's enjoy a cup of coffee now that today's business has been completed."

"Thank you, Mrs. Young," Kyna said politely, exchanging a questioning look with Lenore as the older woman turned to her secretary, who had already prepared a tray and come in to place it on the table.

"Please call me Barbara." The woman dismissed her secretary and poured the coffee herself. "And may I call you by your first names?"

"Of course," Lenore said, beaming, her natural ebullience returning upon discovering that the formidable Mrs. Young was not so formidable, after all. "You're certainly not anything like we expected."

Kyna hoped her partner wouldn't elaborate further, but as she listened to the other two women exchange conversation, she found she didn't have to worry. Barbara Young not only had a shrewd head for business but enjoyed a highly developed sense of humor. She laughed uproariously at Lenore's embellished assumptions over what kind of woman she'd turn out to be and even added a few comments at her own expense.

By the time they had finished their coffee and were preparing to leave, the three of them were talking like old friends. They walked out of Barbara Young's office with the feeling that it wouldn't be long before they had a lease for the original space they had coveted with attractive terms. Barbara had even extended an invitation to a meeting of a local merchants association being held in a downtown hotel toward the end of the week.

"Was it my imagination, or is that woman the fairy godmother we had in mind?" Lenore asked once they were inside Kyna's Volkswagen and driving toward the boutique.

"If not, she came awfully close," Kyna admitted, still in a state of shock. Lenore's inquiry ignited a questioning spark inside her head she couldn't seem to dispel. There had been an enchanted quality to her life for the last three days. She had danced with a handsome Prince Charming, been given hope for the future by a fairy godmother, and it all seemed too good to be true. "Where are the ugly stepsisters in this piece?"

She didn't know she had spoken aloud until Lenore laughed. "Probably waiting for us at the Gilded Lily. Everyone knows our clothes can make anyone look good."

Distracted by her fanciful thoughts, Kyna barely acknowledged Lenore's joke. She shook her head. "Lenore, did Mrs. Young remind you of anyone?"

"Santa Claus dressed in a Dior suit and reeking of old money," Lenore proclaimed, then began babbling enthusiastically about the wonderful future opening up for them. "In a few years, we'll be able to hire an efficient store manager and some good salespeople; then you and I can flit off to the Riviera and spend all our fabulous money."

"We won't become jet setters on forty thousand a year." Kyna grinned, her smile fading as another possibility occurred to her. "We'll draw a nice salary only if the new store does as well as we've projected. If it doesn't, we'll be worse off than we are right now. And remember, Mrs. Young can still turn us down."

"Don't even think it!" Lenore raised an accusing finger. "We're under a lucky star, Kyna. We can't lose."

"Hope so," Kyna murmured distantly before they both lapsed into silence, each occupied with thoughts of the future.

Kyna was kept very busy over the next two weeks; nevertheless, she thought a lot about Blade Maddox. Would he ever call her again? As the days passed, she was forced to acknowledge he had written her off, and even though she had suspected that he had lost interest in her after their date, it still hurt. Perhaps he expected his women to fall into bed with him first thing and didn't plan to waste more time on her because she had put him off.

At the end of the week and with still no word from Blade, Kyna learned that the penthouse was occupied solely by Rod Williams, who gave out word through the grapevine that he was back in circulation. One morning she spoke with the loquacious Mrs. Levine while they shared the elevator and learned that Blade had recently taken possession of his new house. Kyna was angry with herself for being upset over hearing the news secondhand. After all, she and Blade had only dated once, and he had made no promises, so why should she care what he did? But she did care; she couldn't get him out of her mind.

That night she was unable to sleep. Lying in bed, as she'd done a number of times over the past weeks, she tried to recall every detail of her night out with Blade. He had been complimentary, charming, an interesting dinner companion, and he seemed to have enjoyed her company as much as she did his, so why hadn't he contacted her again? She had never experienced such a powerful attraction to a man, but evidently the feeling was not returned.

She could almost see the tawny gold strands of his hair layered back from his temples, his clearly etched profile, ruggedly handsome. She could feel the caramel warmth of his appreciative gaze on her skin, the contractions in her lower body as those eyes caressed her figure. He was lithe and hard, with broad shoulders and muscular limbs. Whenever she'd looked at him, she'd felt an exciting sizzle along her nerve endings, an inexplicable surge in her pulse rate. "Think about work," she commanded out loud, forcing his image out of her mind.

The designer they had contacted to consider doing the interiors for the Gilded Lily had come up with some impressive ideas, showing that the concepts they had in mind could one day become an impressive reality. It was Barbara Young who had called to recommend Hubbard Design, leading Kyna to believe that the signing of the lease was almost a formality. The friendly developer was showing more than a passing interest in tenants not yet signed, and Kyna was still uncertain why. She and Lenore had been treated like honored guests at the meeting Barbara had invited them to attend. She made sure they met all the right people and gave them the opportunity to hear some sound advice in retailing by long-established merchants.

Odd as it seemed, Kyna and Barbara Young enjoyed an instant rapport. At times, Kyna wondered if Barbara's avid interest in their business stemmed from a developer's worry that they were too inexperienced to know what they were doing, but eventually, after several phone calls and two luncheons during which business was not even discussed, she'd decided that the woman simply liked her. She felt lucky to have such a knowledgeable friend and wondered why she, instead of Lenore, had fostered what was almost a motherly interest. Still thinking about it, Kyna finally fell asleep.

Hours later, the strident ringing of the phone somewhere near her left ear brought her groggily awake. Struggling to open her eyes, she reached for her alarm clock. "It's after two!" she gasped, untangling herself from the sheets as she grabbed for the phone. Had something happened to her parents? Lenore?

When she heard the steady breathing as she grappled with the receiver, she was afraid she might be the victim of an obscene caller, so when she finally gathered the courage to speak, her voice came out in a cracked whisper. "Hello?"

"Kyna? Kyna O'Brien?" Blade's deep voice jolted her to complete wakefulness. Why on earth was he calling her? Especially at two in the morning? Maybe she had been lucky to be rid of him for as long as she had, for this was out of line.

"Yes?" she declared suspiciously, trying to sound as if she couldn't place the voice.

"Damn these European connections," Blade exclaimed loudly. "You sound strange. This is Blade. Can you hear me?"

With the receiver held an inch away from her ear, she said shortly, "Stop shouting! What do you want?" So he was in Europe, was he? That still didn't mean he had the right to wake her up in the middle of the night.

There was a noticeable pause before he came back in a much softer tone, the caressing inflection that sent hot shivers over her skin. "I want to know how you've been."

"Fine." It was all she could think of to say, refusing to give in to the pleasure she felt at the sound of his voice. When he didn't offer anything else, her temper rose. What was he expecting? Did he think she'd reveal how often she'd thought about him over the last few weeks? How upset she'd been when he hadn't called? "Is that all?"

"What?" He sounded slightly hurt; then a comprehending sigh echoed through the receiver. "It's after hours there, isn't it? I'm drinking café au lait and munching a giant croissant. What are you doing?"

"I'm lying in bed talking on the phone to an idiot," she announced waspishly, pushed even further out of sorts by his unwavering good humor.

"That conjures up a nice picture in my mind."

She could almost imagine his teasing smile and retorted, "I hope this transatlantic call is costing you a fortune, because you woke me up out of a sound sleep and scared me half to death. I thought you were a heavy breather."

"I can't get that aroused by phone," Blade reassured suggestively. "But I'll be back on Sunday."

Ignoring the fluttering sensation in her stomach, Kyna asked, "From where?"

"From Paris. My flight gets in Sunday night. Can you pick me up at the airport?"

Kyna couldn't believe he'd make such a request and wriggled to an upright position, propping herself up against the headboard as she brushed her tangled hair away from her eyes. "Let me get this straight," she intoned curtly. "You're calling me from some swank hotel in Paris at two in the morning in order to ask me to meet your flight?"

"I'd appreciate it, sweetheart," Blade admitted, the seductive quality still present in his voice. "You'll come, won't you?"

"Who do you think you are?" Kyna was outraged. She wasn't falling for his latest pitch any more than she had to the other practiced lines he'd used on her. "I'm not your personal taxi service. Why don't you call a woman who's seen you once or twice in the last two weeks?"

"Because you're the only woman I want." He refused to be put off, continuing the conversation in the same flirtatious vein. "I'll have to remember that you're cranky when you first wake up. It might come in handy later on. I've been out of town all week, and before that, I was arranging the move to my house. Between the decorator, the plumber and the electricians, I've been up to my neck in details, but on Sunday I'm free."

"Good for you," Kyna said ungraciously. "But that doesn't explain why I should drop everything and go to pick you up at the airport."

"I'd like you to be the first person to see my house," Blade stated smoothly. "I want to prove that my preferences don't lean toward red lights, undulating beds and fur rugs."

"I'll take your word for it," Kyna obliged sarcastically. "Now I'm going back to sleep. Good-by, Blade."

"Kyna!"

"What?"

There was a significant pause; then Blade said gruffly, as if he were having difficulty finding the right words, "I've missed you, Kyna. It seems like years since I last saw you. I really do want you to be the first person I see when I get off the plane."

She could hear his intake of breath, waiting for her to say something, and when she didn't, he continued swiftly, "I'm being honest, Kyna. Please believe me."

There was no mistaking his sigh of relief when she gave in and inquired, "What flight?"

When he gave her the details on where to meet him, the self-possessed demeanor she distrusted in him was entirely absent. Before much more was said, a crackling interference came over the wire. "I've given you two weeks to think things over, Kyna. Has that been slow enough for you?" Blade asked, a boyishly pleading inflection in his voice.

Before Kyna could form an appropriate answer, the line went dead. Slowly, she replaced the phone. "It certainly was," she whispered, vastly relieved he couldn't hear her acknowledgment. He was conceited enough as it was. He also had a real talent for preventing her sleep. She had to stop letting him affect her like that.

Getting out of bed, she put on her pink velour robe

and tied the sash tightly at her waist. She had almost resigned herself to never seeing Blade again, but with one impertinent phone call, he had her pacing her apartment in total confusion, unable to think about anything else. Maybe she was a fool to rush out and meet his plane when he'd done nothing to deserve such consideration, but for some reason she'd found she couldn't turn down his request, not after he'd contritely convinced her he honestly wanted to see her again. Perhaps the man had cast some kind of spell over her, for she wasn't usually so easily manipulated.

Marching to the kitchen, she heated herself a cup of warm milk. When it reached the right temperature, she laced it with honey and carried the mug back to her bedroom. Sipping the sweet concoction, she waited for it to make her drowsy. Eventually, she closed her eyes and drifted asleep, only to dream of magnificent white chargers, golden-haired kings and gilded lily petals strewn at her feet.

6

At his first sight of Kyna, Blade paused in his passage through the enclosed gate. She hadn't spotted him yet and didn't look as if she were trying very hard to locate him. She was leaning casually against a white pillar, gazing out the large airport windows as if more interested in the outgoing flight of some jet than in seeing him again. Although that bothered him more than he'd like to think, he was glad of the chance to get his fill of looking at her before she spied him.

She was wearing the kind of clinging dress he liked on other women but, oddly enough, didn't on her. Glancing around, he noticed that several male occupants waiting on other passengers were admiring the shape of her long legs, full breasts and small waist. He usually deliberately associated himself with decorative women, so why did it trouble him to know other men found Kyna desirable? He wouldn't want her so badly if she didn't have a curvaceous figure, innocent face but seductive green eyes, would he?

He thought back to the last two weeks, when he'd deliberately stayed away from her, supposedly playing things her way but aware he might have been attempting to punish her for refusing what other women rarely denied him. Maybe that was why he wanted her so much. On Kyna, the honeyed charm that seemed almost second nature to him had little effect; the harder he pressed, the more she mistrusted him. Why was he so drawn to a woman who didn't fit his life style, demanded more from him than he wanted to give? Why did he feel an unexpected urge to protect her? What was wrong with him, anyway?

An irritated furrow developed between his brows. He'd dated several beautiful women since that night out with Kyna but found he didn't want to make love to any of them. No, a leggy green-eyed brunette had gotten under his skin, and he wouldn't be satisfied until he'd had her in his bed and proved to himself she was no different from any other woman.

He began walking toward her, willing her to turn toward him, to demonstrate how much she longed to see him again and show those watching that she was only interested in him. It was hard to disguise his temper when she finally noticed his approach and did nothing, merely waited for him to reach her side without saying a word. Refusing to acknowledge that his behavior was prompted by a painful dent to his ego, the kind he'd suffered more than once since they'd met, he placed his briefcase down on the floor and abruptly pulled her into his arms.

Kyna's astonished lips were parted by his scorching mouth. Caught off guard, she stumbled against him, and he immediately drew her even closer against the solid strength of his chest. Like a lover who had been away too long, he expressed his joy at having her back in his arms, kissing her as if he needed to slake the thirst of long separation. She abandoned herself to the joy of physical intimacy with him, forgetting where they were, forgetting everything as his tongue demanded she join in his play. The feel of his large hands on her back, pressing her against him, was exactly what she craved, had craved for weeks.

The sound of a jet engine firing up for takeoff broke the spell, and Kyna stiffened in Blade's arms. She knew that by coming to meet him she was agreeing to a deeper involvement with him, but she never expected him to stake his claim in public.

"Blade?" she whispered, when he finally let go of her and bent down to pick up his case.

"Everyone else was doing it." He took her arm, his expression far more casual than what was implied by his kiss. "Look around. I didn't want to be the only man without someone to kiss hello."

"That was hello?" Kyna asked, hoping he wouldn't notice the trembling in her legs as they proceeded up the concourse.

An odd expression came into his eyes, as if he'd experienced some kind of self-revelation that both pleased and troubled him. His crooked grin was disarming. "Maybe I put more into it to make up for the many times I've come off a flight and didn't have anyone waiting for me. I'm glad you came, Kyna. Very glad."

Was the loneliness she sensed in him for real? From what he'd told her of his background, she'd assumed he'd had a happy childhood. He had a mother who loved him very much, a stepfather whom he liked and respected, so why did he make it sound as if no one cared for him? She'd supposed he satisfied himself with short-term affairs, demanding few commitments, but maybe he had re-evaluated his life and was telling her he didn't intend their relationship to be that meaningless, that she represented more than another willing woman to satisfy, temporarily, his needs in bed.

Without thinking what it might signify to him, she slipped her hand into his and smiled up at him. "I'm glad, too."

He didn't let go of her hand until they reached baggage claim. After picking up his luggage, they made their way through the terminal, transversed the parking garage and stowed his bags in the trunk of her Volkswagen. "Do you think I'll fit?" He eyed the small bug doubtfully.

"Your chauffeur didn't think to bring the Rolls," she teased, making a dramatic show of opening the passenger door.

She pinned a serious expression on her face as he dutifully coiled his long body into the car but felt it slip when she noticed that his knees were jammed uncomfortably against the dash.

"I probably deserve this." Blade shrugged ruefully, rolling down the window so he could lean one arm along its edge. "At least it's not too far to my house. I won't have to suffer long."

"A short penance is usually more meaningful," Kyna quipped, then swiftly strode around to the driver's side and got in. "I'll have you home in no time. That is, if you give me good directions."

He proceeded in doing exactly that, and they were soon driving west on the outerbelt. As she maneuvered the small car between lanes, she could feel his warm gaze on her, as if he were embracing her with his eyes and found she wasn't nearly as immune to such tactics as she'd hoped. If she didn't do something to dispel the sexual tension strung out between them, she feared she'd end up driving right off the road.

"Were you in Europe on business?" she inquired, taking great effort to make her smile appear casual.

"We're thinking about introducing some American retailing concepts into foreign markets," Blade supplied vaguely, looking as if he would have preferred conversing on any other subject.

"Retail markets?" Kyna didn't take the hint, curiosity fostering another question. "I thought your company's main interest was in real estate? What does that have to do with retailing?"

"We're a diversified company." Blade shrugged, forcing an end to the conversation by saying, "If you don't mind, I'd rather not talk about business. That's all I've done for seven days."

"All right," Kyna said, understanding how he might feel that way. "What would you like to talk about?"

"You," he challenged softly; then, noting her closed expression, he changed course. "Or how you're doing at the Gilded Lily."

Unlike him, she didn't mind talking business and enthusiastically relayed all that had occurred since the last time she'd seen him. She described her growing friendship with Barbara Young, telling him how much she admired the woman and how grateful she was to her for considering them as tenants. "If we get that lease, we'll have done everything on our own without seeking help from anyone." Kyna's smile was self-satisfied. "You don't know how important that is to me. I was afraid I'd have to slink home and admit defeat, but not only did we get the loan, but it looks like we'll get a lease for the space we wanted in the mall."

Blade's expression was strange, and at first she thought she'd gone on too long about something that didn't concern him, but his question discounted that worry. "Independence isn't all that it's cracked up to be, Kyna. I once thought so but discovered almost too late that everyone needs help sometime."

"I'm not a fanatic about it." Kyna laughed, not catching his relieved expression as she located their exit and drove up the ramp. "I'm just happy we've got something to show for all our hard work. All Barbara seems to care about is our bottom line."

"You call her Barbara?" Blade sounded surprised.

"I told you," Kyna explained, "we've become friends. You'd like her, Blade. She's a fantastic lady."

"So I've been told." Blade cleared his throat, then pointed at an upcoming sign. "This is our turn. The area isn't very well lit, so we'd better shelve our conversation until we reach the house."

Ten minutes later, they were parked in front of a large modern home facing the Scioto River. The exterior was done in rough cedar shakes, the low-angled roof in black slate. An architect's dream, the multilevel house fit in perfectly with its natural setting, appearing almost part of the cliffs cut from the limestone banks of the river. Kyna admired the contemporary lines, which somehow blended with the landscape of jutting rock and tall trees.

"Wait until you see the inside," Blade enthused, struggling out of the car. He was swiftly around to her side, assisting her to her feet. With long strides, he drew her along with him to the double doors that faced the circular drive. "I'll come out and get my luggage later."

Once inside, she quickly learned that Blade's taste wasn't anything like his friend Rod's. She highly approved of the spacious interior, the eclectic blend of modern and antique furnishings. Blade seemed most proud of the cedar decks juxtaposed off the kitchen, master bedroom and living room. As soon as they'd finished touring the interior, he asked her if she'd mind fixing him a sandwich while he went out to the car and collected his luggage, then took a fast shower and changed clothes.

Knowing how many hours he had spent on a plane, Kyna readily agreed and walked into the kitchen as he headed for the front door. The kitchen was as efficiently designed as the rest of his house. Its black and white decor was boldly masculine but not austere. A center skylight softened the effect of stark colors, and hanging plants enhanced the feeling of warmth. Spotting a coffee maker, Kyna searched and quickly found his supply of coffee and started a pot. While it was brewing, she searched through his almost-empty refrigerator until she found a packet of cheese and cold cuts. Although she would have preferred making him something a little more solid, he seemed pleased with the meager fare when he joined her after completing his shower.

He had exchanged his business suit for a white oxford shirt, yellow golf sweater and a pair of close-fitting brown cords. She served him at the large white bar, taking the stool next to him so she could enjoy the cup of coffee she had poured for herself. While he wolfed down his sandwiches and drank several cups of coffee, she drank in her fill of the sight of him. It had been so long, and he looked so good.

"All that caffeine's not good for you," she advised, but he didn't appear worried.

"I've waited too long to see you again and refuse to fall asleep while you're here." Looking down at his

empty plate, he patted his stomach, then complimented her. "That was great."

"Baloney," Kyna argued, groaning when he refused to credit her pun.

"One of my favorite foods," he enthused, holding
out his hand to her as he slid off his stool. When she
was on her feet beside him, he pulled her through the
patio's glass double doors off the living room so she
could look out over the river and see how cleverly the
architect had provided a different scene from each
standpoint.

"It's lovely, Blade," Kyna complimented, leaning
over the rail so she could see the gentle waves come
up on the gravel shore. "I'd adore living in a house
like this." Realizing how her words could be taken,
Kyna avoided Blade's eyes, pointing to the lights that
were flickering across the river from the opposite
shore. "You must spend hours out here enjoying the
view."

"It is beautiful out here at night, but the wind is
coming up. Come inside." He reached for her hand,
gently leading her back inside. His smile was tender,
drawing her to him almost as much as his compelling
gaze. It was as if the gold flecks in his dark eyes were
burning a welcome to her, and she was guided by
them to the wide oatmeal-colored couch. She didn't
protest when Blade softened the lights by turning a
switch on the wall. She could tell by the hunger in his
dark gaze that he wanted her and that he knew she
wanted him, too.

"If we sit here, we can look out on the river. It's very
relaxing, and we can still enjoy the view," Blade
remarked nonchalantly, but his eyes were telling her
he would seek beauty in other places. He watched her
take her seat but remained standing, smiling down at
her.

One part of her was aware that she shouldn't just meekly follow his lead, but another part yearned to give in to the caressing velvet in his voice, longed to feel his warm breath on her fevered skin. Her green eyes darkened with desire when he shrugged out of his sweater and unbuttoned the top two buttons of his shirt to reveal his tanned throat.

He was going to make love to her; she knew it but also knew she wouldn't do anything to prevent it. The two weeks she had spent without him had heightened, not dampened, her desire for him. The old saying "Out of sight, out of mind" couldn't have been farther from the truth.

He lowered himself on the couch, sliding one arm around her shoulders as he pointed out the window with the other. Awareness of him became almost a physical pain, the sound of his low voice increasing the ache. "If you look over there, you can see where the water starts churning from the dam. There's a full moon, so you can make out the white foam."

Try as she might, all she could see was their intimate reflection in the glass doors, his cheek inches away from the black veil of her hair, his arm resting lightly on her shoulders, his thigh pressed against hers. "Can you see the dam from here?" she inquired, crossing her legs to break the searing contact with his thigh that was taking her breath away. She saw by their reflection that she'd only succeeded in drawing his attention to the provocative slit at the side of her gray silk skirt, and she could feel his dark eyes on her legs like a caress. The anticipation was already overwhelming, but he increased the torment by placing one finger along the enticing sliver of exposed thigh. "It's a warm night," he murmured, ignoring her question and lightly stroking a teasing pattern on the thin hose covering her leg. "Might be one of the last until spring."

She could barely manage a nod, a crazy, tingling excitement shooting through her veins. She had no thoughts of stopping him, and even had she wanted to by wetting her lips, her mouth couldn't form a single word. His fingers had inserted themselves beneath the slitted silk and were slowly feathering higher as he leaned closer, edging her shoulders farther and farther down on the couch. The rough texture of the cushions rubbed through the silk of her dress, and she became aware that all of her senses were becoming ultrasensitive, her body tuned to a fever pitch of excitement. Before completely losing her balance, she reached out with her hand, but her fingers clutched the material of his shirt, pulling him with her as she fell sideways on the cushions.

Blade was alongside her in an instant, his lips curved in a gentle smile as he surveyed her flushed face. "What are you telling me with those mysterious eyes, Kyna? Do you want me to touch you?" He lifted a silken length of her hair, letting the luxurious dark strands slip through his fingers. "Ebony shimmers," he whispered thickly. "I love the feel of it in my hands."

"Blade, I—" Kyna made a tiny movement that brought a taming hand to her hip, but she had no thought of backing away from the pleasure to come.

His warm fingers played intoxicating games with the hem of her skirt, sliding the smooth silk up and down her quivering thighs, while his sherry-gold eyes seduced her and molten honey fell from his lips. "How I want you, green eyes. There's no mouth that softens so completely beneath mine, no aphrodisiac more powerful than the fragrance of your skin, no breasts as perfect for my hands."

When his mouth slowly lowered over her lips, she was far past questioning his sincerity, paralyzed by anticipation, crying out for him to possess each part of her he'd mentioned. The first light contact was far too soft and brief to do anything but prolong the agony; she needed more, much more. Lifting her arms, her fingers clutched in his hair, and she pulled his mouth back to hers, moaning with pleasure when he complied with several of her ardent wishes all at once. He pressed down on her, thigh to thigh, hip to hip, then slid his arm beneath her until her breasts were crushed against his chest. His kiss was a feast of passion, filling her mouth with searing promises and fierce demands.

She felt the throbbing aggression in him and clung to him, satisfying the same aggression in herself. His fingers sought the buttons of her dress, easily separating the two halves of her bodice, then widening the gap so he could touch the satin-covered mounds beneath. Through the smooth material, she was tantalized by the feel of his fingers rubbing over her nipples. The erotic sensation inflamed her, and she writhed beneath him, demanding he soothe the craving he had fostered within her. His kisses made an intoxicating passage from her lips to her throat, then down to the soft skin of her breasts. The thin straps of her slip prevented him from pleasuring more than the top halves of the twin curves, but she didn't know if she could stand a full assault just yet. His warm mouth sliding across her flesh set off another explosion of reaction through her. A combination of kisses, nips and flicks of his tongue and she was arching her back, kittenish moans telling him of her need.

With trembling fingers, she undid the remaining buttons on his shirt, sliding the white cotton off his shoulders and down his arms. The feel of hard muscle, smooth flesh and crisp chest hair excited her further, and she pushed herself lower so her lips could gather the same impressions as her hands.

"Kyna," Blade groaned as an involuntary shudder

rippled the broad expanse between his flat nipples, "I can't stand much more of this without taking you."

"I know," Kyna whispered, kissing the taut skin along his ribs, her fingers gently teasing inside his tight waistband.

"God, you're a torment," he said hoarsely, forcing himself away from her. "You're a combination of innocence and passion no man could resist." He was standing up and looking down at her a few seconds later. Before saying anything, he pulled his shirt off his wrists, then bent down and lifted her off the couch. His brown eyes were ablaze with gold as they centered on her swollen lips, then caressed the delicate skin of her cheeks and finally locked with the passionate green tide beneath her lush lashes. "Will you come with me, Kyna? Will you stop this ache I have inside me?"

"Yes, Blade," she promised, tracing the short golden strands of hair at his nape with her fingertips. She pressed her cheek against his bare shoulder and placed her palm over his heart.

He carried her to the suspended spiral staircase, seemingly unaware of her weight as he swiftly ascended the stairs. At the top, he lowered her feet to the thick cream carpeting, then brought his hands to her shoulders. As she gazed into his eyes, he slowly swept her silky black hair behind her back, then eased the silk dress from her shoulders. Standing before him in her lace slip, she sucked in her breath as he pulled the straps down her arms. Encouraged by the adoring look in his eyes, she stepped out of the slip and removed her pantyhose and undergarments, strangely proud of her nakedness as his gaze warmed her feminine curves.

"I've dreamed of you, Kyna," Blade murmured. "Dreamed you'd come to me someday, but no dream could capture such beauty."

Standing motionless before him, her eyes reflected her own dreams as her golden-haired king stepped back and removed his clothes. She couldn't articulate her feelings as he had done, but they duplicated his words. The reality of Blade was more exciting than any dream. Draped in autumn moonlight, his skin shone like gold. There was strength, vitality and splendor in each shimmering plane of lithe male flesh. Feeling as if she might explode, Kyna watched him, her breath coming in short pants. Her eyes adored his hard, muscled chest, swept down the line of tawny hair that crept down his flat stomach, came to rest on his thighs, taut with power. His obvious desire for her brought a heated flush to her cheeks, darkened her eyes and parted her lips. Woman to man, they confessed the age-old longing that seemed to gather more strength with each passing second. The air vibrated between them, creating music without notes, a harmony played on strings of desire.

Blade held out his hand, and Kyna placed hers into it. In slow motion, they walked together to the massive wood canopied bed. With one swift movement of his arm, Blade pulled away the cream-colored linen spread, then turned to her, lifting her up briefly, before placing her down on the white sheets. Bending over her, he spread her hair across the smooth, down-filled bolster, sifting the shiny black strands between his fingers. Kyna closed her eyes, blocking all stimuli but the feel of Blade's hands in her hair.

Expecting him to lie beside her, Kyna gasped when she felt his hands running lightly down her legs. At the foot of the bed, Blade knelt alongside her knees, smoothing the soft skin of her thighs and stomach. "So beautiful," he whispered, and began a fiery trail of kisses from ankle to thigh.

Ever so slowly, he caressed up her long legs, kissing,

stroking, teasing, until an overpowering urgency built in her and she reached out for him, her fingers digging into the smooth flesh of his shoulders. "Please, Blade," she whispered frantically, pulling him down to her.

Covered by his strength, Kyna's arms slid around his waist, her hands stroking restlessly up and down his taut spine. His lips tasted her sweet moans of longing, which blended with his own as he parted her thighs with one knee, wanting to be one with her. They were fused together by a fulfilling surge of pleasure that catapulted them both to unbelievable heights. He activated the soaring tension within her higher and higher until she became a wild thing in his arms, demanding, then giving of herself until she became the catalyst that detonated the final wondrous explosion that shattered them both.

Entwined with his body, Kyna patterned his descent back to reality, breast to breast, hip to hip, thigh to thigh. They shared the floating aftermath, even as they'd risen together toward a summit neither of them had reached before. "You were everything, Kyna," Blade mumbled into her hair. "Everything I knew you'd be."

To her, his words were the perfect description of what had been a startling revelation. It was he who was everything, he who inspired her to give all she had to offer, yet took nothing away. Numbly, she listened to the slowing rhythm of his heart, overcome by feelings that were far too new, too strange to put into words. Was this love? Was it the finest passion a woman could feel for a man, or was it simply the outcome of being with an experienced lover who was an expert at pleasing women? If it were the latter, she didn't want to know, didn't want to ruin what, to her, had been so special.

She could sense that he was waiting for her to say something, but what could she say? I love you for this moment, Blade, but tomorrow I might feel differently? Do you feel this way with any woman or only with me? Knowing she could say neither of those things, she lifted her head slightly off the pillow and placed a gentle kiss on his temple, her fingers tenderly stroking his hair away from his forehead. If he could read what was in her eyes, he would know what she was feeling, and he did see something there, for when he looked at her, his gaze was golden warm.

Taking her with him, he rolled to his side, kissing her gently. He began a second journey, much different from the first but just as wonderful. By the time they'd climbed to the lofty heights again, her questions were lost, scattered into floating silver particles that drifted off with the moonlight.

7

I have to go now, Blade," Kyna whispered, not wanting to wake him if he had fallen asleep. She needn't have worried, for his response was immediate.

"Are you crazy, Kyna?" He propped himself up on the bed, his brown eyes intense. "It's after four in the morning. I'm not letting you drive back to your apartment this late."

"I have to go to work in the morning," Kyna reminded him matter-of-factly, then, spying a short robe on a nearby chair, got out of bed and slipped it on. The silky fabric, slithering against her skin, helped cool her still-overheated senses as she began gathering her clothes up off the floor. "Don't worry about me. Go back to sleep."

"I don't want—you're not going anywhere," Blade pronounced, catching up with her before she made it to the bathroom. "Come back to bed, Kyna. I'll take you home in the morning."

She was taken aback by his stern expression. "That would be silly, Blade. Besides, I'll need my car."

"I'll take care of you, honey." Blade smiled indulgently. "You don't have to worry. In the morning, I'll take you wherever you have to go."

The words he used sounded almost like the ones her father had spoken to her on more occasions than she could count. If it had been left up to him, she wouldn't have formed a partnership with Lenore, wouldn't be living alone in the city, wouldn't even have gotten her driver's license. She'd been protected from "worry" all of her life, and it had almost crippled her. She loved her independence and wasn't about to let Blade decide what was best for her.

Sensing her unwillingness to comply with his wishes, Blade reached for her hand. "You don't really want to go, do you?" Pulling her close against his naked body, he lowered his head and kissed her. Kyna couldn't help responding to him and slipped her arms around his neck, kissing him back. Taking her pliancy as agreement, he lifted her off her feet and began backtracking toward the bed.

Thinking the matter was settled, he placed her down on the mattress, then came down beside her. "You won't need this," he assured tenderly, attempting to slide the robe down her shoulders. "I want to feel your body beside me all night."

Ignoring the renewed longing that immediately rekindled inside her, Kyna shook her head, clutching her fingers in the lapels of the robe to prevent him from removing it farther. "Blade," she protested, repeating her argument, "I'll need my own car tomorrow, so you can't drive me home. I've got a full schedule, several people to see and must get an early start. I'm going."

The gold flames that sparked in his eyes were not caused by desire. "You really mean that, don't you?" he inquired tightly.

"Yes, I do," Kyna declared firmly, a small frown starting up on her brow when she saw that he was getting angry. "I've stayed far too long as it is."

He seemed to be wrestling with some internal quandary. "What does that mean? Are you looking at this as some kind of one-night stand?"

"Why would you ask such an insulting question?" Kyna cried, stunned that he could misjudge her so badly. "Is that what you think?"

"I think you're having second thoughts and want to get out of here before you have reason for more. You knew what was going to happen when you agreed to meet me, so why are you running out?"

"My reasons for leaving have nothing to do with my feelings for you, and you should know it." Kyna tried to get off the bed again, but he caught her wrists before she could stand up. "You don't own me, Blade. Let go of me."

Their gazes locked, each determined to have their own way. Blade was the first to back down. He released his hold on her, raking one hand through his hair as he watched her stand up from the bed. "I may not own you, Kyna, but I do worry about you. I don't like thinking of you out on the road this late at night, and I blame myself for not coming up with a better plan for this evening. I'm sorry I said what I did. I'm just not used to dealing with a woman who means this much to me. I want more from this relationship than good sex. I want to take care of you."

"Thank you." Kyna lifted her clothes from where

she'd dropped them when he'd kissed her. "I appreciate your concern, but there's no need. If I had known this was going to upset you, I would have left earlier."

They both were aware that she couldn't have left earlier if her life had depended on it, but apparently Blade didn't feel it was a good time to remind her. However, he did remind her of something else. "Does it upset you to hear that I want you body and soul? That I want to protect you? You sidestepped those comments very neatly."

"You can plan all you like, Blade." Kyna walked swiftly back toward the bathroom. "But unless I agree, nothing will come of it, will it?"

"Kyna! Why are you—"

She shut the door before she could hear the rest of his question. Closing her eyes, she leaned her head against the mirror over the sink, ashamed of herself for cutting him off in midsentence, for saying something so nasty to him after the wondrous time they had shared. The scent of his body emanated from his robe, and a sharp pain of longing began in her chest. Quickly, she stripped off his robe and stepped into the shower.

The cold spray stinging her hot skin was exactly what she needed to numb her conflicting thoughts. She didn't want to think about the implications of her behavior that evening, didn't want to think about the interpretations he had put on it. There was too much going on in her life then to consider making even more changes, adding more complications. After she'd done what she'd set out to do, made the Gilded Lily into a financial success, then she'd have time to build a lasting relationship with a man. So what did that make that night if not the one-night stand he'd described?

Stepping out of the shower, Kyna dressed quickly,

the last question she'd asked herself increasing the guilt she already felt for so completely giving in to her desire for him. Blade had said that his previous sexual relationships were superficial, but where she was concerned, he wanted more. On their first date, she had told him she expected more from him, yet when he implied he was offering something deeper, she'd immediately backed off. Could she make him understand that it was the wrong time in her life for her to accept all that he was offering?

It was going to be dawn in a few more hours, and she knew she wouldn't find answers to her questions until she'd had sufficient time to think, time away from him. Usually happiest when she was most busy, she now found herself regretting the full agenda she'd scheduled for herself all week. The first leg of her race to success might be won in a few more hours if her meeting with Barbara Young meant that the woman had decided to grant them a lease.

At the moment, all she really wanted to do was walk back into the bedroom and tell Blade she was his for as long as he wanted her. Of course I don't want to do that, she berated herself silently, realizing she was no longer certain what she really wanted to do about anything. That night, she'd reshuffled all of her priorities and was terrified she'd never be able to categorize them neatly again. Why couldn't Blade Maddox have stepped into her life at some other time? Sometime in the future, after the Gilded Lily was on its feet and showing a healthy profit?

Taking several more minutes to compose herself, she finally found the courage to re-enter the bedroom, but her defensive thoughts were written across her face. "You don't have to look like that, Kyna." Blade made no attempt to come near her, even though he'd gotten dressed and had been waiting for her to finish with her shower. "I may not like it, but I'd rather send you home than lose you altogether."

Making no comment on that, Kyna forced herself to smile. Seeing it, he shrugged and walked over to where she was standing. "That's what you were thinking about in there, wasn't it?"

Kyna shook her head. "I'm too tired to think, Blade. I'll call you as soon as I get home so you can get some sleep."

He walked her outside to her car; then he kissed her good night, and the tender assault on her lips was almost her undoing. She was half-blinded by tears as she maneuvered her car out of the driveway but was driving slow enough that he couldn't see what a difficult time she was having. In the rear-view mirror, she caught sight of him standing at the open door, watching her, and sensed he would go on looking long after she'd driven out of his sight.

Once she'd arrived at her apartment, she made the phone call, not surprised when he picked up the receiver after only one ring. They didn't exchange more than a few words, and minutes after she'd hung up the phone, she was asleep.

Her alarm went off at seven, and even though she felt as if she'd barely closed her eyes, she rolled groggily out of bed and got dressed. Twenty minutes later, the image reflected back to her from the mirror was that of a sophisticated career woman. She looked very chic in the short, fitted cognac suede jacket, worn over a matching straight skirt. A green blouse framed the slender line of her throat with a short stand-up collar and highlighted her large eyes. She had chosen the outfit to make herself appear as if she were ready to face any challenge the day might have to offer, but when she looked in the mirror, all she saw were the faint purple shadows under her eyes that proclaimed her exhaustion.

She realized there was nothing she could do to erase them unless she climbed back into bed, but she couldn't do that without canceling her appointment with Barbara Young. She didn't want to make the slightest misstep that might offend Barbara, especially since the lease for the Gilded Lily was still unsigned.

At eleven, Kyna dragged herself into Barbara Young's office, feeling as if she'd already put in a full day. Jenny had gotten sick and couldn't come to the store, so she'd had to help Lenore on the floor. Also, one of their orders was missing from a stock shipment, and she'd had to hassle the supply house to reissue the merchandise. They were the kind of things she could have easily managed if she'd had enough sleep, but that day such minor problems had her feeling strung out with tension.

"I'll be done here in a minute, Kyna." Barbara pointed to the silver coffee urn on a side table near her desk, then returned her attention to the papers on her desk. "I want to get these out to my secretary so they can be typed up by the end of the day."

"No hurry." Kyna smiled, grateful to have a few minutes to relax before they got into a business discussion. "I'm dying for a cup of coffee."

"Rough morning?" Barbara asked kindly, looking a bit frazzled herself.

"Hectic," Kyna admitted, carrying her coffee to a comfortable leather chair in front of Barbara's desk. "And you?"

"The same." Barbara placed a sheaf of papers into a manila file folder, then leaned back in her chair and stretched her arms over her head. "I've been ready for lunch since before breakfast. Sometimes I yearn for the time when all I'll have to do is lounge around in bed all day."

An immediate picture of Blade and herself lounging in bed appeared in Kyna's head. "That does sound nice," she confirmed, her green eyes shimmering.

Barbara stood up from her desk and slipped on a white nubby-wool jacket over her silk print blouse. "Let's go into the conference room. I've got all my papers in there."

"Have you made a decision, Barbara?" Kyna asked, experiencing a growing sense of elation as she followed the white-suited woman through the paneled door to the adjoining room.

"Yes, I have. Just this morning, as a matter of fact." She flipped open a manila folder and extracted several legal-sized documents. Indicating a chair beside her, she handed one of the copies to Kyna. "Here's the lease for the Gilded Lily. Take a moment to look over the terms and assure yourself that they are as we discussed."

Barely hiding her excitement, Kyna read through the lease and with shaking fingers reached for a pen. "Thank you, Barbara. You must know what this means to Lenore and me."

"You don't have to thank me, dear," Barbara began, but broke off when there was a light tap on a connecting door. "Now what?"

A tall blond figure strolled into the room, his face down as he studied the papers he held in his hand. It was Blade!

"Mother, I need your signature . . ." He glanced about the room, his dark eyes narrowing with surprise when he recognized Kyna. He came to a sudden halt, his words trailing away to nothing.

Across the room, Kyna remained stock-still in her

seat, her mind paralyzed by astonishment and disbelief. There was a rush of sound, a ringing in her ears, and she swayed, reaching out for the edge of the table to steady herself. He couldn't be there, but he was and looked every bit as nonplused as she.

"Blade"—Barbara was the only one who hadn't lost her powers of speech—"I thought you were with a client."

Regaining his composure far faster than Kyna, Blade came farther into the room. Without lowering his eyes from Kyna's pale face, he said, "That meeting is over. I didn't realize you'd be in here with—" He ran an agitated hand through his hair and sighed. "Mother, I need to talk to Kyna. Would you mind leaving us alone for a few minutes?"

"Oh, dear." Barbara's glance moved from one shocked face to the other. "Are you sure you don't want me in here, Blade?"

"I'll handle this," he replied grimly, never taking his eyes from Kyna.

Barbara hurried out of the office, her face suddenly gone as pale as those of the two silent people she left alone in the room. As soon as Kyna heard the loud click of the door closing, she regained her ability to think, to sort out the onslaught of suspicions that washed over her head all at once.

Blade was Barbara's son! Blade knew all about her meeting with George Masters, and immediately thereafter, George experienced a complete turnaround and arranged for her to see Barbara. That day, Barbara had granted their every wish, giving them easy terms, a prime location in the mall. Why? Because she'd been told to do so by her son, now that Kyna had gone to bed with him?

Blade was behind all the wonderful things that had happened to her business and was the reason Barbara had offered such easy terms in their lease. She was now well aware why she and not Lenore had been the subject of Barbara's maternal interest. The woman had been checking her out, trying to decide if Kyna was good enough for her cherished son! And she had thought the woman truly liked her, wanted her as a friend! Well, it was all clear to her now. She thought about the discussion Blade could have had with his mother that morning; he'd probably assured the woman that Kyna suited him well.

"Oh!" Kyna gasped, so angry she felt ready to explode. "You—you—"

"Don't say it," Blade pleaded, holding up his hand. "Not until I've had a chance to explain."

"Explain?" Kyna exclaimed bitterly. "You have an explanation for deceiving me like this? If so, I already know what it is. I can almost hear you talking to your mother about me. Smooth the way for this woman, mom. I don't want her business affairs to interfere with the personal one I'm planning for her."

"I don't need my mother to smooth the way for me, Kyna. If I want a woman, I get her on my own," Blade said as he began moving toward her, walking slowly, as if he feared she might bolt at any second. "Your wanting space in our mall was just a coincidence. You got it because you proved you could be a profitable addition, not because you're having an affair with the developer's son."

"I'm not having an affair with you," Kyna shot back, then, realizing there was no other word to describe her relationship with him, stammered, "At—at least I wasn't until today. You expect me to believe you told Barbara to consider me as just another prospect to fill space at the mall?"

"That's exactly what I did." Blade was much too close, forcing her to look up in order to meet his eyes.

"I know I should have told you who I was, but you were expounding about your independence, and I knew how you'd take it."

"When *were* you going to tell me?" Kyna snapped. "After you'd convinced me to live with you? Wasn't that what you were leading up to this morning? Now I know just what you meant when you said you wanted to take care of me. Well, you certainly have!" She scraped her chair back and bolted upright. "You've been trying to do that since the first day we met!"

She turned on her heel and started for the door, but Blade's hand closed around her arm. "And what's so bad about that?" he bellowed, his voice bouncing off the walls.

"Let go of me," she commanded, her voice deadly quiet. Her slanted green eyes flashed a warning even he couldn't misunderstand, but he refused to let go, dragging her away from the door. He pushed her down onto the chair she'd just vacated. Placing one hand on each arm of her chair, he effectively trapped her.

As he leaned over her, the gold flecks in Blade's eyes burned into her defiant face. "You're staying put until we get this settled! I'm sorry you had to find out like this, but I'm glad it's finally out in the open. No matter what you think, I only wanted to help you, and if you weren't so paranoid about accepting favors, you wouldn't be reacting like this."

"You're the one who's been accepting favors—my favors," Kyna lashed out, pushing against his arms, which felt like steel girders. "I've been treated like a china doll all my life, but I'm a grown woman and don't need someone to take care of me. I can damn well take care of myself."

"Proven by how well you handled yourself on the jogging course?" Reacting to the totally unforgiving look on her face, Blade made a contemptuous sound deep in his throat and grasped her by both arms, pulling her up out of the chair into brutal contact with his chest. "Can you protect yourself from me, from this?"

She twisted her face away, but his fingers wound in her hair, forcing her head back. Just before his lips crashed down on hers, she read the frustrated intent in his eyes, and she whimpered in panic. He swallowed the terrified sound when his mouth imprisoned hers, his tongue thrusting past the barrier of her teeth.

Not content with the sweet bounty he plundered with his lips, he released her hair and began a stroking rampage down her ripe curves. When he reached her breast, his hand slipped inside her jacket. His fingers rapidly undid the buttons of her blouse, robbing her of breath when his large hand lifted the weighty fullness from the cup of her bra, catching her nipple between two fingers. She struggled against the gray fog that was fast closing in on her, but before her legs collapsed beneath her, Blade altered his tactics.

His lips softened, tantalizing the tender curves of her mouth, trying to elicit a response. His hand gentled on her breast, his fingers stroking in all the ways she had already shown she enjoyed. She fought to control her immediate response to him. This man had deceived her, how could she be responding to him? But her body's needs ignored her mind's restraint, and she sagged weakly against him. "No," she murmured softly, even as her lips drank in the taste of him, her hands stealing beneath his jacket as her fingers clutched the material of his shirt.

"Oh, Kyna," he moaned against her lips, then dropped feather-light kisses over her face. "I can't give this up."

"Blade," she whispered, overwhelmed by the resurgence of feeling that had begun the first time they'd made love and enveloped her then. When his lips came back to hers, she kissed him hungrily, taking everything he was capable of giving. Her hands swept over his back, kneading the taut muscles beneath his clothes, holding him close to assuage the want in her body.

Locked together, it took several moments before they were aware that they were no longer alone. Barbara's discreet cough filtered through the haze of desire that surrounded them, and Blade slowly released her.

"It looks like you've settled your differences," Barbara remarked, then, noting Kyna's dishevelment, discreetly turned her attentions to the papers on the conference table while Kyna swiftly readjusted her clothing. "I did knock."

Blocking Kyna from view with his body, Blade faced his mother. "Nothing's been settled yet. Bad timing must run in the family."

Barbara didn't seem in the least perturbed by Blade's curt tone. "I thought you'd prefer me to Paul and several fixture manufacturers. As you know, they've arranged to meet in this room at eleven-thirty." She looked over her shoulder at the clock. "It's almost that time now. Why don't Kyna and I adjourn to your office."

"That won't be necessary, Mrs. Young." Kyna stepped from behind Blade and, mustering as much dignity as possible, walked to the conference table to pick up her purse. She saw the signed lease but made no attempt to pick it up. "I won't hold you to that, considering why you made the offer. I didn't realize that my—my relationship with your son had any bearing on our deal."

Kyna wondered why she'd never made the connec-

tion between Blade and Barbara before, for there was
no doubting the resemblance between them as Barbara's brown eyes flashed with gold. "I knew that's what
you'd think, but surely Blade didn't say that?"
Barbara's glance narrowed on Blade's face, then,
reassured by his negative nod, focused back on Kyna.
"I still think we could have resolved this more easily if I
had stayed in the room."

Slightly intimidated by Barbara's intense frown,
Kyna still didn't relax her rigid stance. "He didn't have
to tell me anything," Kyna said bitterly. "The facts
speak for themselves. If you try to tell me that he had
nothing to do with my getting that lease, I won't
believe it."

"And you shouldn't," Barbara agreed smoothly.
"Blade had everything to do with it."

"Mother!" Blade's appalled exclamation drew both
women's eyes.

"Well, you did," Barbara continued, seemingly
amused by his thunderous expression. "If you hadn't
told me about Kyna's unfortunate experience with
George Masters, her situation would never have come
to my attention."

"But I never asked you to give her that lease,"
Blade stated grimly. "Tell her that, too."

"You didn't have to," Barbara said calmly, ignoring
the muffled curse he made as she strolled around the
table and took Kyna's arm. "Let me explain further,
Kyna. We'll go down to Blade's office, where we can
have some privacy."

Too upset to think properly, Kyna allowed herself to
be guided to the door. It was obvious that Blade was
shocked by his mother's remarks, which proved that
he hadn't deliberately intended to influence her in
leasing space to the Gilded Lily but Kyna saw that,

nevertheless, Barbara had been prompted to consider it because of Blade's interest in her. Her green eyes widened with amazement when Barbara ordered Blade to stay behind in the conference room.

"The hell I will," he exploded, stalking after them to the door, coming to a full stop when his mother spoke sharply.

"You know Paul expects you at his meeting, and after all, Kyna is my concern." There was a strand of steel in Barbara's voice. "It was my decision to grant Kyna a lease; therefore, I will handle any explanations that are necessary."

Kyna was well aware that Blade was still not convinced. A pulse jumped along his jawline, and his hands were clenched at his sides, but he didn't come any closer, astounding Kyna by not challenging his mother's authority. "Very well, Mrs. Young," he said through gritted teeth, his eyes darkening almost to black. His lips were tight when he switched his attention to Kyna. "I'll speak with you later."

Before Kyna could respond to what sounded very much like a threat, Barbara pulled the door shut behind them, firmly closing off further conversation. With a determined stride, she led Kyna down a carpeted hall. "Being president does have its advantages." Barbara stopped before a door embossed with Blade's name. "But I must say, I detest it whenever Blade calls me Mrs. Young. It always means he's furious."

When Kyna didn't offer a comment on that, Barbara's expression became rueful. "I know that you're furious, Kyna. That's why we're going to have this private talk. I value your friendship, and I hope we can get back on a friendly basis. Perhaps you'll understand why I did what I did when you learn more about my association with my son. I'm far more confident I can explain myself to you than I could to him. I'm counting on you to do that for me."

Kyna's brows rose. "Me?" She was now certain Barbara had overestimated her involvement with Blade. "I don't think so, Barbara. You don't understand—"

"Your relationship with my son?" Barbara asked. Kyna nodded and Barbara smiled, then stated cryptically, "I probably understand far better than you think."

8

Blade's office was decorated in a surprisingly conservative style. It looked more fitting for an English barrister of the past than a modern, American businessman. Comfortable cordovan upholstered chairs, supple with age, were grouped around a massive roll-top desk. Gilt-framed hunting prints hung on the dark paneled walls. A large oriental rug covered the varnished oak floors and added to the hushed ambience of the room.

Above the mantel of the marble fireplace hung an impressive portrait of a man appearing to be in his late sixties. Seated on a brass-studded leather wing back, the white-haired man rested one hand on the head of a liver-and-white-colored springer spaniel. The man's distinctive brown eyes were smiling, denying the serious expression on his rugged face. It could have been a much older version of Blade, and Kyna found herself staring.

"That's my father," Barbara informed, taking a seat near the fireplace. "I see you've noticed the resemblance to Blade." She laughed up at the picture. "He's like his grandfather in other ways, too. Sometimes I really regret that my father didn't have the opportunity to get close to Blade. I'm sure he could have helped me understand several things about Blade I almost learned too late." As if ridding herself of some disturbing memories, Barbara shook her head. "Enough about my family for now. We're here to discuss your business. Why don't you make yourself comfortable, Kyna. Please have a chair."

Kyna sat down, folding her hands in her lap as she faced the feminine woman, who appeared to be right at home in the masculine office. Barbara smiled, then began. "It's true that it was Blade's interest in you that prompted me to look into the matter. He told me about your meeting with George, so not only did I feel I owed it to you to rectify that situation, but I wanted to meet the woman who had inspired Blade's concern. I'll also admit that after meeting you, I wanted to get to know you better for reasons that were unrelated to your financial status. Perhaps that wasn't fair to you or to Blade."

"Why did you want to get to know me better?" Kyna asked, thinking she already knew the answer but needing to hear the explanation from Barbara's own lips. She tried to hide her hurt feelings, keeping her expression calm so Barbara wouldn't see that she felt betrayed by both Barbara and her son. Blade had interfered in her business, but Barbara had befriended her only to satisfy herself that Kyna was a suitable choice of woman for her son.

"You reminded me of myself," Barbara surprised her by saying. "I could sense your ambition, your pride in your work, and I wanted to offer whatever encouragement I could. I know how hard it is to build up a business, and soon after we met, I knew that you were determined to succeed. I thoroughly enjoyed our conversations. Listening to you brought back memories of when I was first starting out on the same road. There're not many women who reach out for what they want with your single-minded resolve."

Seeing a crack in Kyna's emotionless expression, Barbara pressed. "Kyna, the decision to grant you that lease was based on my intuition. Putting together what I'd learned about you with the encouraging figures provided in your pro forma, I decided to give you a chance, even though it's a decided risk."

Crossing her legs, Kyna leaned slightly back in her chair and folded her arms across her chest. Her short laugh was almost resigned. "First Blade pulled a few strings out of personal concern for me, then you grant me a lease because of your intuition about my ambitious nature. I would have liked to have been credited as a shrewd professional who represented a sound business. There's hardly much satisfaction in attaining the lease this way."

"This may sound cynical, but strings are pulled in most business deals. The old adage that it's who you know and not what you know is quite true. You're very naive if you think that's not so, and you'd be a fool if you turned down a business opportunity because it's offered as a personal favor." Barbara leaned forward until her intent gaze forced Kyna to meet her eyes, eyes so much like Blade's that Kyna was hypnotized by the warmth in their dark brown depths. In a softer voice, Barbara elaborated. "Kyna, everyone needs help getting a business started, and if you're as smart as I think you are, you'll take advantage of this chance. Granting you a lease can only assure you a prime location. The ultimate success of your business is up to you and your partner. That's where you'll gain the satisfaction of proving yourself."

"Perhaps I should be more grateful for the lease even if we didn't get it for the reasons I wanted. I agree that Lenore and I have to take it from here, but it still galls me to know that we've received special treatment because of my personal relationship with the developer's son."

"Why, Kyna? Why are you so adamant about becoming a success without accepting any favors from people who want to help you?"

Kyna couldn't answer immediately, her gaze drifting away from Barbara's to stare sightlessly at the floor. When her voice came, it was hushed, almost choking in her throat. "Maybe because I've had too many favors thrown my way for all the wrong reasons. My parents are older and believe that women have no business in the working world. They didn't even approve of my going to college, and certainly not to one that would take me away from home. They took care of all of my needs and wanted to go on doing it until I found a suitable man to take their place."

Unable to remain seated, she rose and crossed to the heavily draped window beyond Blade's desk, her hand restlessly toying with the sheer underdrape. "I don't like it, but there's always been someone trying to protect me, offering me things I haven't earned. First my family, now you and Blade. When Lenore and I started the Gilded Lily, it was the first thing I'd ever set out to do on my own. My partner and I are very proud of what we've accomplished so far, and I don't want anyone granting favors they don't feel we deserve."

Anxious to convey her position, Kyna blurted out her real feelings, feelings she knew weren't completely shared by her business partner. "I need to prove to myself that I can make it without help."

"How ironic," Barbara intoned softly. "You may not realize it, but you and Blade have a great deal in common."

Kyna turned around. "How can you say that? He's told me how you made him start at the bottom of the ladder and work himself up, that he had to work hard and justify his position with the company."

"True." Barbara nodded. "He proved himself just as you want to do. Perhaps that's why he wanted to help you. When he started here, he had to live on the salary we paid every other member of our junior staff. Even though I'm his mother, he earned his place here. It wasn't easy, and it won't be easy for you, but that doesn't mean he didn't require some help."

Kyna read the sincerity in Barbara's eyes and knew she was telling the truth. "Then he should certainly understand how I feel. Why didn't he tell me you were his mother or ask me if I wanted him to get involved in my situation?"

Barbara smiled. "Perhaps he was afraid you'd take off in the other direction. This need you have to be totally independent is one of the first things I noticed about you, and I'm sure he's noticed it, too."

"Maybe," Kyna conceded, still not completely convinced. "Or perhaps he hoped to solve my business problems so they wouldn't complicate our personal relationship. I probably shouldn't say this, but I don't think Blade's interest in me runs very deep."

"And I probably shouldn't be telling you this, but I know Blade's a lot more interested in you than he's evidently let on. I've concluded that not so much by what he's said but by what he hasn't said. I'm really sorry things happened this way. I'm certain Blade meant to tell you everything in his own time. He was just waiting for the right moment."

"And I know exactly what kind of moment he'd

choose," Kyna muttered under her breath, her cheeks flaming when she saw that Barbara had heard her.

Barbara's brown eyes were twinkling with amusement. "I'm almost positive Blade didn't dare admit he was part of Palmer & Young until he felt more secure about your feelings. You're not the kind of woman he's used to, Kyna. He's probably aware you can offer him much more than the previous women in his life, and he's trying his best not to scare you off until he decides on the best way to deal with that."

Kyna's disagreement with that assumption was far too vehement, once again imparting much more information than she intended as she began pacing back and forth in front of the window. "But Blade doesn't want any more from me than he gets from any other women in his life. Wasn't what you witnessed this morning proof of that?"

"From what you've just told me, that didn't resolve things between you. The attraction you're both experiencing only compounds the issue. You've offered Blade quite a challenge, Kyna. If I know him, his next step will be to shower you with flowers and expensive presents, and I'm almost certain they will influence you even less than his kisses. I can hardly wait to see how the two of you work this out."

"Barbara!" Kyna was shocked.

"Please sit back down, Kyna," Barbara invited with a throaty chuckle. "I'm going to have to recarpet Blade's office if the two of you don't reach some kind of understanding one of these days. Try to be patient. I know my son very well, and unfortunately I'm partly responsible for some of his faulty thinking."

She waited for Kyna to return to the chair she had vacated before elaborating. "When Blade was growing up, I was so caught up in building my career that I didn't give him the attention he deserved. The lesson he learned was that money could buy love, for it was really only money that he got from me. I bought him whatever he asked for and didn't realize what I had done to him until he was out of college and expected me to hand over the company."

A lingering sadness gathered in Barbara's eyes. "I did an abrupt about-face and almost lost him. Over the years, we've developed a better relationship, but it still isn't all I'd like it to be. As far as business is concerned, Blade and I know where we stand, but our personal relationship still rests on slightly unsteady ground."

Kyna reached across the space and caught Barbara's delicate hand in her own, empathizing with her because she felt the same uncertainty where Blade was concerned. "At the moment, I'm not sure where I stand with him, either. But I do know I don't want him to think I'm going to agree with everything he says or does just because I enjoy his kisses."

"What *are* you talking about?" Blade demanded angrily, striding into the room without preamble. "I thought this discussion was supposed to be about the lease. What have you been telling her, mother?" He threw the papers he was carrying down on his desk, then leaned back against it, facing the two women, who appeared to be chatting like old friends before the fireplace.

Barbara was far more adept at circumventing her son's temper than Kyna. Even after what the woman had told Kyna about her relationship with Blade, she didn't appear to be in the least intimidated by his towering aggression but rose to her feet and walked regally to the door. "Why don't you take Kyna to lunch? She can tell you whatever she feels you should know."

"Well?" Blade inquired, his casual tone dangerously

deceptive. "Did you agree to keep the lease, or didn't you?"

"Yes, I did," Kyna stated smoothly, providing him with a cool emerald stare, completely overlooking the fact that he might have overheard too much when he'd barged into the office. "And I found Barbara's method of convincing me far more effective than yours."

"Which makes me wonder why you bothered telling her you enjoy my kisses," Blade shot back, a muscle leaping in his cheek. "I thought you were the one who wanted to ensure your association with Palmer & Young was strictly business."

"As far as I'm concerned, it is," Kyna insisted, reaching for her purse as she stood up from the chair. "All my future dealings will go through the proper channels. I'm sure neither you nor your mother will have to involve yourself further unless I default on my lease."

A derisive expression came into his eyes. "And what about our personal involvement? We've already diverted from proper channels there, haven't we?"

Kyna refused to be baited. "Maybe *I* have," she corrected, "but I'm sure you've been operating on your usual course."

At first, he looked taken aback; then his handsome features tightened with suspicion. His eyes burned into her face. "What did my mother do, give you a list of names?"

"What?" It was Kyna's turn to be nonplused.

"I know you weren't discussing business when I came in. Was my mother warning you about my reputation?"

"Hardly," Kyna pronounced. "That warning came from you." She walked to the door. "You can mail me a copy of my lease." She intended to duplicate his mother's regal exit, but his soft voice stopped her as her hand closed around the brass knob.

"I haven't signed it—yet."

Tossing her long hair over one shoulder, she whirled around and took a few steps toward him. "I don't expect you to sign it. I want only one more favor from you, Blade."

"You're actually requesting a favor? My, my, quite a change since this morning." He took a step toward her, his brown eyes glowing as they skimmed over her features, then dropped to the curves of her breasts. "Just what did you have in mind?" he asked, his voice taking on a low, husky quality.

Kyna's eyes were like green shields withstanding his sensual challenge. "All I want you to do is convey a message to your mother. Tell her she can send the lease to the Gilded Lily."

"She doesn't have to be bothered any further with this," Blade informed silkily. "I can sign it; it's on my desk right now."

"I'm not doing business with you," Kyna snapped, her temper flaring. "I'm doing business with your mother!"

"But I can do much more for you than my mother," Blade insisted mockingly. He had been taking slow, measured steps toward her, and Kyna had unconsciously been backing away. With her shoulder blades pressed against the door, there was no way to curtail his advance, but she wouldn't willingly be victimized again.

"I know you enjoy my kisses, and unless you're a terrific actress, you enjoy everything else I can do for you." Their eyes clashed in a battle of wills that Kyna knew she couldn't afford to lose.

His movements were slow, cautious, but she was well aware of his intent. Holding her gaze, he lifted one arm and tenderly grazed her cheek with his hand before pressing his palm against the door. She amazed herself by not flinching away from his touch. His other hand was soon in the same position on the opposite side of her head, and his breath was warm on her face. "Our business together isn't over; it's just starting."

"Stop it, Blade!" Kyna ordered, feeling the familiar sensual tension beginning to build within her. "This didn't work the last time, and it won't work now. If you want to convince me we should go on seeing each other, you'll let me go."

"That hardly makes sense," Blade drawled, a quicksilver smile matching the flashing gold lights in his eyes. "After last night, I don't want to let you go. Not for a long, long time." He tilted his head and kissed her softly on her cheek, then worked his way toward the throbbing pulse near her temple. "You're mine."

"Blade," she protested, knowing if she didn't do something fast, she'd be clinging to him, begging him to continue the tantalizing torment until it reached its inevitable conclusion. When she felt his fingers in her hair, brushing the strands away from her ear so his tongue could have access to the delicate shell, she took a deep breath, commanded her body into action and quickly ducked underneath his outstretched arm. A bit more frantically than she would have liked, she stepped beyond his reach.

"I don't belong to you or anyone!" she cried. "You're smothering me just like—just like—" Her breath was expelled in exasperation. "Damn it, let me out of here."

Whether it was from the desperation in her voice or the emerald anger shooting from her eyes, Blade moved aside. She didn't even look at his face as she ran out the door and had reached her car before she dared slow her pace. Exhaustion from the emotional confrontation coupled with her lack of sleep as she drove toward her apartment in a hazy trance. Once inside her apartment, she called Lenore and told her they had gotten the lease but implied that she wasn't feeling well and wouldn't be coming in for the rest of the day.

Since Kyna was rarely sick and hadn't missed a day of work in over a year, Lenore was concerned, asking if she should call a doctor, but Kyna was finally able to convince her partner that there wasn't anything seriously wrong, that she was simply suffering from total exhaustion. She assured her that with a day's rest she'd be back to her normal self, and finally Lenore believed her.

As soon as she'd hung up the phone, she dragged herself into her bedroom, stripped off her clothes and climbed into bed. She had reached the point where she could no longer think, needing to escape into the silent oblivion of sleep. She pulled the covers over her bare shoulders and effectively closed out the world. The touch of the cool sheets soothed her nerves and eased the terrible pounding in her head.

While the afternoon sun slipped lower in the sky, she lay in a dreamless stupor, not moving. Eventually, daylight was replaced by darkness, stars shafting pale light into the room, and she submerged further into a deep sleep, the restorative sleep of gauzelike dreams and misty fantasy.

Upon a lush mattress of green ferns, she lay in the forest, watching her lover as he stepped from beneath the frothy spray of the secluded waterfall, his wet, naked body caressed by the morning sun. "Blade," she murmured happily, opening her arms to greet him. His dancing brown eyes appreciated every curve of her sun-kissed skin, and he smiled at the provocative movements she made to him with her body as she enticed him to come and lie with her on the soft, natural bed. There was no way to suppress her joy when he knelt at her feet, then bent over her, his bronzed flesh glistening with moisture.

Her eyes worshiped the hard muscles that rippled beneath his skin, growing dark with passion as they moved down his smooth shoulders, his golden brown chest, then lower. Beneath her lush lashes, she reveled in the knowledge that he was full with wanting her, his tensed thighs providing a background for the aggressive masculinity that beckoned to her. "Come to me, Blade," she demanded softly, smiling at him. "Let me show you how much I want you."

Leaning over her, her lover reached out to stroke her aching breasts, but she didn't want him to touch her, not yet, not until she had shown him all the pleasures she could bestow. She moved her fingers to his chest, tracing the tapered flesh lower and lower until she found him.

His low moan prompted a knowing smile to lift the corners of her soft lips, and she intensified her caress, whispering love words between kisses as she moved her mouth from his ribs to the flat, taut skin of his stomach. The involuntary shudder of muscle thrilled her, aroused her, and her throaty chuckle was met by a challenging low growl.

A pleasurable heat made intrusive inroads into her dream, a textured excitement she could feel from ankle to breast. Her nostrils were assailed by the musky scent of masculine sweat, her body crushed beneath a heavy weight, and she struggled against it. The idyllic haze was lifting, and she fought out of the languor that had gripped her body, reluctantly opening her eyes.

* * *

"Blade!" she cried, staring up into his face, panicked by the unbridled desire that flared in his eyes. He was real, not her dream lover but the real man who had inspired the fantasy!

At the sound of her voice, Blade lost all control. Wild with need for her, he was desperate for the taste of her. Her slender body, squirming beneath him, had pushed him farther and farther into the vortex of desire she had aroused with her soft fingers and even softer mouth. He took her lips with the ruthless hunger of a man on the edge of explosive passion. His tongue thrust past her lips, seeking the melted honey taste he would find within her. Showing her he would not be content with the wild gifts she had given, he returned them, kiss for kiss, stroke for stroke.

Her whimpers of delight spurred him on, and he slid lower, grazing her slender curves with his mouth until he reached the tender flesh at the inside of her thighs. He rewarded her for the unexpected seduction she had offered to him by bringing her to the shuddering precipice of frenzy, then retreating until she was crying out to him, begging him to take her, as far gone in passion as he had been when he had felt her moist parted lips on his skin.

Crazed by the flooding white-hot pleasure that enveloped her, Kyna was unaware that her frantic movements had brought him to the point where he could no longer control his own need. Pushing her shoulders down on the mattress, he lowered his weight upon her, grasping her hips as he sought entry. Kyna arched her back, wrapping her legs around his, meeting him, needing him to take her.

Still, he prolonged the pleasurable torture, entering her so slowly that she moaned with insatiable longing. Measure by measure, he filled her, then rested, deepening his possession with agonizing surges that she thought might go on forever, until the final repeated onslaughts that drove them both toward soul-shattering culmination.

They moved together like light focused on a common source. Kyna couldn't think, could only feel, unwilling to relinquish the unity that brought the shuddering release of passion. There was only the two of them clinging to one another as the brilliance radiated, then slowly faded in intensity, until they lay still, completely spent.

Blade rested over her, his legs entwined with hers. His breathing was ragged, hot against her skin, until he regained enough strength to move his weight to one side so she could catch her breath. Awareness returned slowly, but when it did, all of Kyna's concentration was centered on the very real presence that lay possessively close to her naked body.

She refused to open her eyes, knowing if she did, she would have to admit that she wasn't lying on a bed of fragrant ferns. There wasn't a private waterfall a few yards beyond their bed, and bright rays that warmed her bare skin were not being filtered through the tall trees of a secluded tropical rain forest but through the sheer curtains at her bedroom window.

What have I done? she inwardly screamed, but the answer was as fleeting as the dream that had destroyed all of her inhibitions and created the paradise now erased by a cataclysmic reality.

9

H-how did you get in here?" Kyna lay stiffly at Blade's side, unable to deny the pleasure they had just shared together but distraught by how he had taken advantage of her vulnerability. She had thought herself alone, safe from Blade's compelling presence . . . "How long have you been here?"

Clutching at the sheet to hide her nakedness, she jerked up into a seated position. The clock on her bedside table registered six A.M. She had slept through an entire afternoon and night! "Blade!" She shook his shoulder, demanding he open his eyes and explain exactly how he'd managed to end up in bed with her when the day before she had stormed out of his office, more angry with him than ever before.

"Let me rest for another hour or so, honey," Blade muttered sleepily. "I'm beat, and your bed is far more comfortable than that couch in the living room." He rolled over onto his side, his warm hand sliding beneath the sheet to span her bare waist. "Come here and keep me warm."

"I will not!" Kyna pronounced irately. "I want an explanation for this, and I want it now."

The low growl he made sounded more annoyed than apologetic, which caused an immediate reaction. Kyna forgot her own part in advancing their lovemaking and began to blame him for the entire affair. No matter that she had enjoyed it as much as he had; he shouldn't have trespassed into her apartment, shouldn't have been inside her bedroom when she beckoned to her dream lover. The flush of temper rose on her cheeks, and her green eyes flashed dangerously.

When he didn't make the slightest effort to answer her, she reached across to where he burrowed his blond head into her lace-edged pillow and yanked a lock of his hair. "Don't you dare fall asleep."

Satisfied by his muffled yelp of pain, she wasn't prepared for his retaliation. Within seconds, she was pinned beneath his naked body, staring open-mouthed into his face. His quick reaction was not at all what she wanted and certainly not what she had expected.

She wriggled beneath him, trying to escape, but the slow grin that spread across his face and the response of his body warned her where her movements could lead. She went rigid beneath him, but her heavy breathing thrust her breasts rhythmically against his chest, and his expression revealed his enjoyment of her plight.

"I suggest you learn a better way of getting my attention, woman," Blade warned, the mocking gold flecks in his eyes like miniature explosions of light. "That hurt, but this is much better." He fit his body more heavily over hers, nuzzling her throat. Ignoring the tantalizing feel of his mouth on her skin, the tensed virility of him, she frantically renewed her efforts to escape.

Hardly able to breathe under his crushing weight, Kyna still managed to free her arms and tried to push him off her by digging her palms into his shoulders. When that had little effect, she pinched his side, enraged by how easily he could physically overpower her and how close he was to reigniting their passion.

"Ouch!" he complained in an offended tone. His fingers immediately clamped around her wrists as he forced both of her arms over her head and kept them there by enclosing both of her hands in one of his. "Is that any way to treat a man who's spent half the night worried sick about you and the other half cramped up on your short couch?"

Mistaking the green glitter in her eyes for something other than anger, he brought his free hand up to caress her throat, making it more difficult for her to speak. She let her eyes do her talking for her but grew increasingly frustrated when he continued to misunderstand her mood. "Imagine what I thought when I called the store and Lenore told me you were too sick to make it back to the office. When I called here, there was no answer."

She softened slightly when she heard the anxiety in his tone as he recalled the events that had transpired since he'd last seen her. "I imagined you unconscious or in pain, unable to get to the phone. Maybe you had suffered an attack of appendicitis or something. The longer I thought about it, the more concerned I became, so I called Rod. He wasn't home. That's when I dropped everything and drove over here."

He glanced away from her parted lips only long enough to nod at the phone near the bed. "I plugged it back in after I used my passkey to open the door and had assured myself you were only sleeping."

"T—trespassing!" Kyna choked, angrily shifting her thighs until she felt what her frantic movements were doing to him. She immediately went limp beneath him, blushing when his mouth curved into a knowing grin.

"What do you expect after that warm welcome you gave me?" he teased, maneuvering himself so she could breathe but keeping her in place by locking one powerful thigh over her legs and retaining his firm hold on her wrists.

"I didn't even know it was you," Kyna declared shortly, finally comprehending what had gone on while she had slept the day away, but she was still incensed. "You took advantage of me."

His laughter was totally male, completely self-assured. "As I remember it, you called out my name, begged me to come to you, then did all sorts of delicious things to my body. If anyone was taken by surprise, it was me."

He dropped a light kiss on her mutinous lips. "I had just finished a quick shower and intended to go back to the office to finish some of the work I had left behind on my desk. I knew you'd be angry if you woke up and found out I'd busted in, because I wasn't entirely convinced you could take care of yourself."

She felt an unwanted pull on her feminine senses when his smile tilted at a rueful angle, making his expression a touch boyish and much too endearing. "I sure never expected you to forgive me in such a thoroughly delightful way."

"I haven't forgiven you," she retorted, but knew that her anger was slowly escaping her grasp. The first break in her defensive armor had been made by his engaging smile, and the crack was enlarged by the velvety soft color in his dark eyes as he gazed down at her face. "You're an arrogant, fast-talking male chauvinist, and—and you deceived me. You never told me you were vice-president of Palmer & Young or that Barbara was your mother." Once the accusations started, they wouldn't stop until she'd said it all. "You lied to me. Let me make a total fool out of myself and interfered in things that are absolutely none of your business."

Suddenly, she was free as he let go of her wrists and moved away, sitting up in bed, then reaching across her and effortlessly pulling her up on the bed beside him. "And you've *got* to stop manhandling me all the time!"

He cocked his brow at her. "You've certainly changed your tune over the last hour. I think I liked it better when you told me how you felt about me without words." He lowered his eyes, probing the edges of the sheet, draped over her full breasts. "Can't we go back to that means of communication?"

More vulnerable to that kind of proposal than she cared to think, Kyna folded her arms defensively over her chest, hoping he had missed seeing how swiftly her nipples sprang to life beneath his heated gaze. "We have to talk, Blade. You don't understand how I feel."

"What's to understand?" Blade inquired, ending the visual caress of her body but refusing to let go of her eyes. He shrugged one shoulder away from the headboard and lifted her chin with two fingers. "You're in love with me," he stated seriously, his eyes smoldering as they scanned her suddenly pale face.

His intense regard seemed almost impersonal as he watched the play of emotions storm over her features. She appeared to be stunned. Her eyes were washed by a tide of glacial green that was swiftly melted by dark smoke until they became two large pools of shimmering confusion. Her lower lip dropped but was immediately pulled between her small white teeth, and she started nibbling at the tender flesh. "Aren't you?" he pressed, willing her to deny it if she could but appearing confident she could not.

It was that look of total assurance on his cleanly etched features that threw her. Did he know something she had not yet admitted to herself? "Why do you think so?" She evaded answering his question by asking some questions of her own. "Haven't you heard a word of what I've been saying?"

"I understand that I've developed an image problem where you're concerned, but since you love me, you'll find a way to make me change." His lips were twitching, but he didn't laugh. "Look how effective your methods have been already."

"Since I love you!" Kyna repeated numbly, scowling at him. "My methods? I don't have the slightest idea what you're talking about, and I've never said I love you."

"Yes, you did."

"When?"

"The last time was—let's see." He glanced at an imaginary watch on his wrist. "About an hour ago."

Not quite certain he couldn't be telling the truth, Kyna covered her face with her hands. She might very well have said those words to him while they made love. She could have said anything! What was he doing to her? She felt as if she were sitting dangerously close to a land mine about to explode in her face.

"Look at me, Kyna." His tone was soft but brooked no disobedience. "Don't be frightened of admitting how you feel. I've waited all of my life for someone like you."

"Oh, Blade," Kyna cried, part of her yearning to

say exactly what he wanted to hear but still too fearful of the consequences. Maybe she did love him, but what kind of changes would that mean in her life? Could the life style she had determined for herself accommodate a demanding man like him? He was never far from her thoughts, never out of her dreams. Was that what it was like to be in love? She didn't like it if it was. There was so much she had left to do to establish her business, and she couldn't afford to let anyone stand in her way. Besides, could she truly love a man who had manipulated her from the beginning, who angered her constantly, who didn't react to anything as she wanted him to?

"I don't know how I feel," she cried out, feeling the same turmoil that had driven her out of his office the day before, the same conflicting thoughts she had tried to escape through sleep.

"Don't worry about it," Blade reassured tenderly, taking both of her hands in his. "We've got plenty of time to work everything out. I'll tread softly until you're ready."

"Ready for what?" Her eyes flew to his face.

"Ready to make a commitment." He dropped her hands and rolled to one side, then completely off the bed. "In the meantime, it's a beautiful morning. Let's go jogging. I've wanted to go running with you for the longest time."

Greatly relieved by the sudden switch in subject, Kyna still watched in disbelief as he marched naked to her dresser and began pulling open the drawers until he located what he wanted. With a triumphant exclamation, he lifted out a baggy pair of shorts that had a drawstring waist. Fascinated, she watched as he pulled them up his muscular legs, feeling a bit chagrined that he was able to fit into them at all.

He grinned at her offended face. "Men's hips are

slimmer than women's, but these are damned tight at the waist." He inserted a finger into the waistband and pulled until the white strings were drawn inside the stretchy material. "Breathing might be a problem, but running with you, I'll have that trouble, anyway. Do you have an old sweatshirt you don't care if I ruin, or do you want me to go outside like this?"

He made a suggestive movement of his hips that took her breath away, and he knew what she was thinking, for his smile was a flash of pure male enjoyment. Shaking her head, Kyna smiled back. "Even though you would definitely give the women in this neighborhood a thrill, we can't go jogging. No matter what you think, your shoulders won't fit into one of my sweatshirts, and you don't have any shoes."

He obviously hadn't thought about his feet and frowned down at his bare toes. Then a light went on in his eyes, his enthusiasm rapidly becoming infectious. "Get dressed for running. I'll be right back."

"Blade!" She dragged the sheets with her as she scrambled off the bed, but he was out of her apartment before she reached the bedroom door. What would people think if they saw him dashing out of her place wearing nothing but a pair of her shorts? The man was impossible and had absolutely no modesty. Trying not to trip over the dangling end of the sheet, she made it to the door and peeped outside. The orange light above the elevator told her that he was ascending to the penthouse. Having a good idea what he intended to do, she retraced her steps to the bedroom and started getting dressed. It *was* a beautiful morning, and she needed the exercise, didn't she?

"Someone should have you arrested for breaking and entering." She was wearing a pink jogging suit and waiting for him when he used his passkey to re-enter her apartment. "Being landlord doesn't give you the right to walk into any apartment you please."

"I only use the key for your place." Blade strode to the couch and pulled her to her feet. "Rod let me in as soon as I buzzed from the elevator. I might occasionally overstep my rights where you're concerned, but you don't want me pining away for you inside some prison, do you?"

"It might be good for you to pine a little," Kyna said, trying to hide her pleasure at the sight of him. Still wearing her shorts, his slim hips captured her attention, and her eyes were drawn down his long, muscular legs. He was wearing a pair of white jogging shoes without socks, and she found herself entranced by the shape of his calves and ankles. Rod had loaned him a ragged T-shirt, the arms cut off to expose his powerful biceps. "You're going to freeze to death, and you'll get blisters if you run without socks."

Before he could comment, another thought struck her, and she groaned. "What did Rod say when you showed up with nothing on but a pair of ladies' shorts?"

"Not a thing." Blade grinned, shrugging his shoulders. "I guess he didn't find the situation particularly unusual. Even though you can't tell these shorts belong to a woman, I sometimes wonder about that guy."

"Sometimes I wonder about you," Kyna retorted. "If anyone saw you running out of here, I'll—I'll—"

"No one saw me," Blade assured, tugging her with him to the door. "Come on; let's go outside before the rest of the world starts waking up."

They were inside the elevator, going down, before Kyna risked talking again. The last thing she wanted was to provide more gossip about her and the new landlord. She had had a difficult enough time living down that embarrassing episode in the lobby two weeks earlier, a story that somehow had managed to spread throughout the entire building. "I don't know how you talked me into this. It's going to be cold out there."

"We'll get warm as soon as we start running and get the blood circulating." Blade tucked her hand beneath his arm, so she could feel that he wasn't suffering from the cold, even though he was dressed for summer. "One look at you in that cute pink outfit and I'm warm as toast."

Her dubious snort was mixed up with a surge of pleasure at the compliment. "Blisters will wipe that grin off your face, and don't expect me to tend to them like I did when your knee gave out. I'm not going to be late for work today."

They had reached the lobby, and he was rushing her out the doors. "Too bad. That would have been a great way to spend the rest of the morning. Last time, you escaped out of my clutches, but this time I bet I could convince you to stay."

"Don't be too sure." She laughed, but the words were engulfed by a gust of wind that whipped her hair across her face. Blade's hands were there to smooth the black strands away from her cheeks. He bent his head and placed a hard kiss on her lips.

"I'm sure." His eyes were sparkling, but he didn't wait for her to make another comeback, pulling her with him as he started running down the street. By the time they were nearing the bicycle trail along the river, Kyna was eager to prove that she was in just as good condition as he was, even though she had a much shorter stride. Putting on a burst of speed, she sped down a grassy incline, cut between the familiar trees and reached the blacktopped path several moments before he arrived.

"What took you so long?" she inquired playfully, impatiently tapping her foot on the ground.

His eyes flickered to the softness of her breasts, noting their breathless motion with an explicit grin. "Why hurry when I was enjoying such a nice view. I can't decide which side of you I enjoy watching more, front or back."

"I think you're just out of shape and couldn't keep up with me," Kyna taunted, twirling around and running swiftly away from him again.

The wind lifted her ebony hair, and it beckoned him to follow her. Her soft laughter was captured in the breeze and floated back to him as she rounded a sharp curve in the path and shot out of sight. Not a man to back away from a challenge, Blade picked up his pace, confident he could catch up with her as soon as he'd run around the curve, but when he got a clear view ahead, she was nowhere in sight.

He didn't know whether to stop and look for her in the shrubbery beside the path or run faster in case she had disappeared around the next corner in the trail. "Kyna?" he called hesitantly, not sure she wasn't trying to pay him back for his behavior the morning they had met. He scanned the thick underbrush for a flash of pink but didn't see a sign of her and decided she could run much faster than he thought. Jogging was supposed to be done at an even pace, but she was obviously asking for a race. Shrugging, he grinned at the thought of what he'd do when he caught up with her and started to run, going faster and faster until the sweat started pouring down his forehead and trickling down his chest.

At the top of the last hill, before the trail turned back toward the residential streets, he was panting with exertion, scanning the surrounding area for a sign of her and experiencing several sensations all at once:

anxiety that something had happened to her, irritation that she was playing some kind of trick on him and fatigue from running much faster than he'd done in months.

"Damn it, woman. Where the hell are you?" he muttered, grasping his knees and bending over at the waist in order to catch his breath.

"Enjoying the view." Kyna giggled, sauntering slowly up the hill behind him. "And trying to decide which side of you I enjoy watching most, front or back."

Without getting back to an erect position, he charged like an angry bull. "You little devil," he bellowed, catching her around the waist and lifting her over his shoulder. He carried her off the path on the side of the river, but before he could place her back on her feet, his foot caught on the root of a tree, and they both started falling, landing painlessly on the soft, grassy bank that inclined toward the slow-moving water. Gasping for breath, Kyna rolled down several feet of embankment before her progress was halted by a heavy weight on one shoulder.

The sun was blotted out by the dark shadow of Blade's head as he pinned her shoulders to the ground and gazed down at her laughing face. "You can start paying for all the blisters I've now got on my feet," he growled, not revealing if he was truly irritated or just teasing until he continued. "I can see several things I want, but what do you plan to offer?"

"A halfhearted apology?" she suggested hopefully.

"Not enough." He frowned fiercely, his eyes scanning several other options she had available to her.

"A warm breakfast?"

"I plan to steal that." He twisted his hand in her hair, playfully tugging at the silky strands.

"Then you can also steal a kiss." She pursed her

lips and squeezed her eyes shut as if ready to suffer from some repulsive ordeal.

"A thought," he whispered, already cupping her chin in his large hand. "But once you start stealing, it's easy to take more . . ." He kissed her lightly. "And more." His tongue tantalized her lips apart. "And more." He delved into her mouth, taking everything she had to give.

She didn't feel the damp cold from the ground soaking her clothes, the frost-edged wind biting through to her skin, for she was going up in flames. His kisses inspired heady sensations, some familiar, some new, as his mouth demanded, teased, took, then gently wooed. His hands added to the complicated texture of his embrace, hungry for the feel of her, awed by the silken smoothness of her soft skin, then eagerly seeking more. They were so involved in experiencing the pleasure that they didn't hear the muffled laughter coming toward them from the path until one shocked early-morning jogger wondered out loud to his companion about the state the world was coming to in a voice that could extinguish a forest fire.

Kyna groaned her dismay, hiding her face in Blade's shoulder as they swiftly sat up. She admired Blade's nonchalance when, fluidly, he got to his feet, casually brushed the dead grass from his bare legs and arms, then offered his hand to her in a gallant gesture as if she were some royal personage who just happened to fall at his feet. Blushing furiously, she was more than willing to reach out for his hand and get away from any curious onlookers as quickly as possible. Gratefully, by the time they had walked up the incline to the path, the people who had noticed their romantic escapade had gone on their way.

Blade's hands swiftly brushed the dead grass and leaves from her hair, then proceeded down her back, ending the service with a quick slap on her behind. "Let's get going. I forgot the dangers of necking in public."

"Mmm," Kyna agreed, her teeth beginning to chatter as the wind iced the moisture on her clothes. "Let's really run. I'm freezing."

"Let's," Blade stated stiffly, goose flesh raising the hair on his legs and arms. "Hang onto my hand. You're not getting away from me again. I'm too cold and tired to chase after you."

They were both shivering badly by the time they made it back to her apartment. As soon as Kyna had closed the door, Blade had pulled the T-shirt over his head and was on his way to the bathroom.

"That's not fair." Kyna ran after him, as anxious for the comfort of a hot shower as he. "You were on top and didn't get all wet."

"You're free to join me," Blade shouted, turning on the spigots in her shower. "I'm sure I'd warm up much faster if you did."

She came to a full stop just inside the bathroom door. Even after all they had recently shared, she still felt shy about sharing the shower with him. She knew what would happen if she did and suddenly was experiencing an onslaught of second thoughts. They were behaving like newlyweds, but she still hadn't made up her mind to get more deeply involved with him. The thought of him naked in the shower brought other more erotic fantasies, and she hesitated. If she joined him, she wouldn't stop to think, merely feel, and she had to consider their relationship in a more rational frame of mind before making any kind of decision about the future. "I'll put on some coffee and make us some juice, but you'd better be out of there when I get back."

She hurried to her closet and slipped out of the wet jogging suit, then pulled on a full-length velour robe.

"If I wasn't dying for my morning coffee, I'd come out there and get you," Blade shouted above the spray from the shower. "Don't start cooking any food. I'll do the honors while you're taking your shower."

"Sounds fair," she shouted back, forcing herself to move swiftly out of range in case he decided to change his mind. She almost ran to the kitchen, making herself concentrate on the familiar tasks she did each morning before work, trying to ignore the disturbing fact that there was a naked man singing love songs to her from the bathroom.

10

~~~~~~~~~~~~~~~~~

During the next few weeks, Kyna found out that Blade's idea of "treading softly" consisted of waiting for her to get off work every night, driving her home, then either taking her out to dinner or helping her make a meal inside her apartment. Inevitably, he would end up spending at least part of the night in her bed, and though Kyna would have loved to spend every night in his arms, waking up to his intoxicating kisses, she refused his practical suggestion that they live together. Her independence was far too dear to her, and she worried that she would lose it if she lived with someone who had as strong a personality as Blade.

Then there was the matter of his protectiveness; at times that was comforting, but she feared it could lead to smothering, the kind of life she had escaped when she'd left home. Although it became more and more difficult to conceive of a life without him, she stalled in making any decision that would tie her even more closely to him.

On a Friday night, Kyna had to work late and called Blade at his office to tell him she would get a ride home with Lenore. Assuming that she wouldn't be seeing Blade, she and Lenore decided to go out for supper. They lost all track of time as they became engrossed in discussing the preliminary design they planned to submit for landlord approval. They spent hours discussing the floor plan, the materials they should choose, what kind of store front they wanted, and the signage required. By the time they arrived at their apartment building, it was well past midnight.

After saying good night to Lenore in the elevator, Kyna wearily unlocked her apartment door and walked in, tossed her purse on the table and kicked off her shoes. She was exhausted and couldn't wait to fall into bed.

"Where the hell have you been?" Blade's voice resounded from the living room.

Whirling around, she found him standing a few yards away, facing her with his hands on his hips. Recovering from shock, Kyna forced herself to sound calm as he came striding to meet her. "I didn't expect to see you tonight. I told you I had to work late."

"You also told me you were so tired you intended to come straight home as soon as you'd locked up."

"I did but was too tired to cook, so Lenore and I went out for dinner."

"You could have had the decency to let me know that," Blade interrupted forcefully. "I came home right after work, prepared a meal for us and then watched your portion get cold while you blithely went out for the evening. I've been worried sick."

It had been a long, exhausting day, and Kyna was in no mood to listen to his unreasonable tirade. "Look, you're not my father! If you planned on fixing dinner here, why didn't you say so when I called you? It works both ways, you know. I didn't know what your plans were!" She scooped up her shoes and started toward her bedroom, having no intention of continuing the argument. "I'm sorry you went to all that trouble, but if you don't mind, I'm very tired and would like to go to bed."

"I do mind." He blocked her exit, a quiet menace in his voice. "It's almost one o'clock in the morning, way past the dinner hour, and you owe me an explanation."

"I owe *you* an explanation? Just who do you think you are?" Exhaustion fled, and Kyna's emerald eyes flashed icy shards.

"The man who's been pacing the floor for the past four hours worrying about you, that's who!"

"Don't shout at me!"

"I'll shout at you if I want to," Blade declared, sounding more and more like an irate parent. "You're not thinking of anyone but yourself!"

Kyna had had enough. It was exactly the kind of emotional scene she had often endured with her parents. However, she was a grown woman and no one had the right to lecture her about her whereabouts. "And that's the way I want it!" she snapped. "I don't owe you a damned thing."

"And just where does that put me, or rather *us?*" Blade demanded, something beside anger present in his intense gaze.

"There isn't any *us!*" Kyna was too caught up in her own anger to realize how he might interpret her cutting remarks. "If I have to answer to you for every second of my time, I want nothing more to do with you."

"I see." Blade turned his back on her and strode to the couch, lifting his jacket off the back. "I thought what we had going for us meant more to you than it obviously does." He hooked his jacket on one thumb and slung it over his shoulder. "You're a damned good actress, Kyna. I really thought you loved me and were just waiting to commit yourself until you were sure it would last. Looks like it lasted little over a month."

"Blade, I never said—"

"Never said you loved me?" Blade cut her off, his long legs quickly carrying him to the door. "Some men are fools, Kyna. They think a woman who goes crazy over them in bed has to have some feeling for them."

The ashen color of his skin told her exactly how much she had hurt him, and she cried, "I do have feelings for you, Blade."

"Right." He put his hand on the doorknob. "You really had me going for a while. You were the first woman who wasn't more attracted to my money than to me. Unfortunately, I've just discovered I'm no better off. The only difference between you and the other women I've known is you didn't make me pay for good sex. You offered it free of charge, but that's all you're offering, isn't it?"

"Blade, I—" Kyna was at a loss, struggling to find the right words. He made her sound cheap, as selfish as the women who had used him in the past, and she had to convince him otherwise.

"Will you marry me, Kyna?" The unfeeling question was shot at her like an accusation.

It was an ultimatum, and she couldn't think. "I—I can't just—"

His harsh laugh drained all color from her cheeks. "You don't have to say it. I already knew your answer, but if you ever need stud service again, please call me. At least I know you'll never cost me a dime, and you're great in bed. The best I've ever had."

He opened the door, but before leaving, he looked over his shoulder, a contemptuous smile curling his lips. "If you recall, I never said I loved you, either, but a man my age who wants children is always on the lookout for a wife. These torrid affairs take a lot of stamina, and I was hoping to take it easy, be a faithful husband . . ." He paused and shrugged. "At least for a while." He was out the door before she could move. She heard the hum from the elevator, but she was paralyzed, staring at the closed door until the tears began to fall. They streamed down her cheeks, blinding her, but compelled her to move. She fled into the bathroom, groped for a box of tissue, then cried until there were no tears left.

Numbed, she walked slowly into her bedroom, stripping off her clothes as she approached the bed. Trying to focus her mind on sleep, she crawled beneath the sheets, but a jumble of emotions precluded any chance she had of escaping reality. She remembered the last time she had tried to run away from her feelings through sleep and trembled. Blade had come to her then and made her face what she could not say by jumping into her fantasy as she made love to him, then making love to her in return. Afterward, he had seemed so certain of her feelings, sure she loved him, but she had still been too afraid to admit it. Her fear, her selfish pride and her short-tempered reaction to his concern for her had driven him away for good.

His last words to her prompted another voice inside her head, a voice that told her she was lucky to have escaped with her pride still intact. Thank God she had never said the words aloud, told him she loved him.

Blade had wanted her to marry him not because he loved her but because he desired a family and wanted children before he got too much older. He had even admitted that he planned to be faithful only "for a while." Her doubt about his ability to form a lasting relationship with a woman was now a firm conviction. As his wife, she would have never been able to trust his fidelity.

Although it had only been minutes since he'd left her, she felt an aching void, an emptiness that brought cold shivers to her body. She was alone, completely on her own to do whatever she wanted, but the knowledge brought no pleasure. Would her body always feel like this? Would she always yearn for the touch of Blade's hands on her skin, the feel of his body protectively wrapped around hers as she fell asleep?

With a muffled groan, she sat up and reached for the blanket at the foot of the bed, pulling it up and under her chin. Its warmth was nothing compared with the warmth of Blade's arms, but that night she had convinced him she didn't love him and never would. On the other hand, he had shown her that their involvement would only have lasted until the first time she discovered him in bed with another woman. The distraught voices inside her head went on and on until Kyna finally stopped listening and closed her eyes.

The morning light was glaring across the bed when Kyna opened her eyes the next day. Her first thought was that it was too bright in the room, which meant she had overslept. She glanced at the clock and moaned. It was past nine. Why hadn't Lenore called her?

Then she remembered it was her Saturday off and relaxed until other more painful thoughts made her stiffen again. Blade was gone. He wouldn't be coming back unless she called for "stud service." A hot flush started at her toes and seared up her body. "Never!" she whispered, swiftly rolling off the bed, which brought back so many sensual memories of the man she must forget.

I don't need him, she told herself grimly. Before Blade, all of her hopes and dreams had been centered on making a success of the business. She came to a decision. She wasn't going to let thoughts of Blade disrupt her plans for the future. I won't even think about him, she vowed silently.

During the next few weeks, however, she found she couldn't keep the promise she made to herself. Of course, she had to tell Lenore what had happened and was grateful when her friend didn't press. Even though she tried to escape her thoughts by working longer hours, she was constantly plagued by thoughts of what might have been. Then, one day when she and Blade had been apart for weeks, she got a phone call from his mother. Barbara requested that Kyna meet her for lunch, an invitation she desperately wanted to refuse but couldn't turn down. Even if she was no longer involved with Blade, Barbara was still the developer, and Kyna couldn't afford to jeopardize their business relationship.

During their lunch, Kyna was relieved that Barbara didn't seem to be interested in anything but business. All they discussed was the construction that would have to be done on the new store, but as they were parting, Barbara delivered a bombshell. She was going to retire on the first of the year, and Blade was already taking over most of the responsibilities of president. Therefore, he would be in charge of any future business between Palmer & Young and the Gilded Lily!

Unwilling to disclose how greatly that information had upset her, Kyna had somehow managed to get through the remainder of their lunch, but by the time she got back to work, she was overwhelmed by a mounting dread. How could she face seeing him again, work with him and not be affected by him? Not beg him to make love to her?

During the day, she lost herself in work, but no matter how often she called herself a fool, her nights were rife with loneliness, an agonizing emptiness that could only be filled by the presence of one man, Blade. What was she going to do when she met him again? How could they behave as if there had never been anything between them? There were others at Palmer & Young who could easily handle her account, so why had Blade taken charge of it? To punish her? To prevent her business from succeeding?

As required in their lease, she had submitted their preliminary design to the landlord, and Barbara had approved it. The next step was to submit the prepared contract documents, which consisted of architectural, mechanical, electrical and structural plans. Did Blade intend to block their progress by refusing to accept their submission? It was three more weeks until the architect would finish the documents, and she would have to present them to Blade. She would have to make sure that there would be absolutely nothing in their plans that could incite his disapproval.

Kyna kept in close contact with the architect, familiarizing herself with every aspect of his work in order to prepare herself for the upcoming meeting with Blade. Finally, the week before Christmas, she arranged a ten A.M. meeting, grateful that she had been channeled through his secretary and hadn't had to speak with Blade himself.

With an almost defiant air, she chose a black crepe dress that molded lovingly to every curve, the fitted skirt ending slightly below the knee. The cowl neck fell in soft folds above her full breasts, emphasizing her graceful neck. A slim gold belt accented her slender waist and matched the gold hoops in her ears. It might be a business meeting, but she knew that she would have to fight constantly against her attraction to him and out of revenge wanted to make sure that he suffered the same fate. Even though they hadn't seen one another for almost two months, she hadn't been able to forget him, and she hoped he'd take one look at her and reveal that he, too, had had difficulty blotting her out of his mind.

She was ushered into his office by his secretary, who explained that her boss had been detained a few moments but would be with her shortly. Kyna used the time to shore up her inner defenses, and when she heard him enter the room from behind her, she had taken one of the chairs near his desk, her legs crossed, her hands resting calmly in her lap. Not rushing, she turned her head, her green eyes meeting his speculative glance without fear.

"Blade"—she acknowledged his arrival—"it's good to see you again."

"It's good to see you." Blade returned the meaningless phrase, his gaze straying to the large portfolio propped beside her chair. "You've brought everything?"

"Yes," she agreed, glad that he wasn't looking at her as he walked across the room to take his place behind the desk. He had never looked better, although she was immediately aware of a change. There was a cool hardness about him that she hadn't seen in him before. He was wearing a vested gray suit with subtle dark stripes, a starched white shirt with expensive gold cuff links and a somber charcoal tie. She was suddenly aware that she was dealing with a high-powered businessman who could make or break her business with one scrawl from his engraved gold pen, and she swallowed hard. This man was not the gregarious charmer she had expected but a no-nonsense executive demanding results. She was not faced with the laughing caramel eyes she was used to but an opaque brown gaze showing undisguised impatience and little interest.

"Would you care to show me the drawings?" He cleared a space on his large desk, then seemed to have a better idea. "We'll have more room over there." He stood up and waited for her to bring the portfolio to the long table at the other side of the room.

No matter how painful it was to her on a personal level, she followed his lead, swiftly opening the leather case on the table and laying out the boards. His questions were curt, to the point, and gave no indication of his feelings. Her answers were equally concise, proving how familiar she was with the architectural terms used to describe the documents. Less than twenty minutes later, she admitted to herself that her worries about his attempting to block progress on construction were completely unfounded.

After calling for coffee, he took her elbow in an impersonal grip and guided her back to her seat. "By my calculations, you should be able to open by the fifteenth of March. I suggest you combine your grand opening with the St. Patrick's Day celebration which occurs every year at the mall. You'll be assured of customers and can probably think of some clever promotional ideas that will coincide with the holiday."

"That's a good idea." Kyna smiled. "And very appropriate. I'm half Irish."

For the first time since he'd walked into the office, his expression changed, softened, and Kyna got the impression he was really looking at her, not through her. He mumbled something unintelligible about stubborn Irishmen, then quickly turned away and strode toward the door in order to relieve his secretary of the tray she was carrying into the room. "No calls, Helen," he directed, and waited for the woman to close his office door before returning to Kyna.

She sensed something new in the air, some yet unspoken challenge she had better be prepared to face. He placed the tray down on the low table between her chair and another, then took the unoccupied seat instead of going back behind his desk. "Would you mind pouring, Kyna?" he asked, a satin coating over the brisk tones he had previously used in their business discussion.

"Not at all," she said smoothly, but it was all she could do not to tremble when she poured them each a cup of coffee, adding both cream and sugar before handing him his cup.

She almost dropped her own saucer as he remarked huskily, "You haven't forgotten how I take it. That's nice to know."

A growing uncertainty began in the pit of her stomach. Was he intending to lead their conversation into the personal, or was he only making small talk so they'd both feel more comfortable when they inevitably had to meet again on opening day? Once or twice as they had been reviewing the drawings, she had sensed that he felt the same kind of strain she was under, but then he would say or do something that showed he was in complete control of himself and totally at ease with their tenant-landlord relationship.

"You haven't called me," he remarked casually, as if he were beginning a discussion on the weather. "I was hoping you would."

She took a sip of coffee, then replaced her cup on the table. "I've been very busy." She needed something to do with her hands that wouldn't result in an accident. Holding the coffee cup was out, so she picked up her purse, but he mistook that for an indication she was preparing to leave.

"It's not polite to run out on a meeting before your landlord decides it's officially over." The laughter was back in his eyes as he stared at her over the rim of his cup. "Or weren't you aware of the protocol in these situations?"

"No, I wasn't." Kyna avoided his probing gaze, smoothing her skirt over her knees, then regretting the action when she stole a glance and saw that his eyes were following the unsteady movement of her hands. She felt overwhelmed by the intangible intimacy that gathered between them and seemed to increase in strength with every passing second. "I know Lenore is waiting to hear how our meeting went."

"I'll bet." His laughter was double-edged, mocking both her and himself. "My mother probably has one ear to the door, as well."

Kyna wanted out. She had found it hard enough to deal with him on a business level, but now that he was reverting back to the man she still wanted with every breath she took, she found it impossible. Without another word, she endured his caressing sidelong glances as he emptied his cup, then said, "If you're finished, I do have several things planned for this afternoon."

"It's almost noon." Blade stood up, walked to the table and looked down at the architectural drawings. "I suggest we have lunch."

"Lunch?" Kyna couldn't keep the note of panic out of her voice.

With his back to her, he leaned over the table as if noticing something that had escaped his attention before. "That's right. We can relax over a nice meal; then I'll come back to the office, sign these and have them sent to your architect."

Although Kyna didn't dare ask him if he were threatening her, that was her understanding. Either she agreed to go out with him, or he wouldn't sign the contract documents. Both of them knew the process. Nothing more would happen until his signature appeared on every one of the drawings.

"As long as I'm not gone too long." Kyna resigned herself to her fate, praying for strength. "I'm ready if you are."

Shortly afterward, they were inside his car, traveling west, toward the river. She didn't say anything until she was certain he was taking her to his home. "I thought you said we were going to lunch."

"We are." His expression didn't change, nor did he change the direction of the car. "I often eat lunch at home. It's relaxing to look out over the river and forget about everything that's going on back at the office."

"And do you often bring guests?" Her suspicions were obvious, and he substantiated them further with his answer.

"Never, but I'm bringing you because I know you'll appreciate the view. The river is frozen at the edges, and the ice is covered by a fine powder of snow. The trees are still glistening from that ice storm we had a few days ago. Almost makes my property look like a fairyland, right out of one of my fonder fantasies."

She cast him a sharp look, but he was concentrating on the road, the ice storm he'd mentioned making driving more difficult as they turned north off the freeway onto a lesser-used road. A huge knot of tension gathered beneath her ribs. One of his fonder fantasies! She recalled how they'd eventually laughed together over her dream, the dream he had unwittingly shared when he'd broken into her apartment. Was he now planning to include her in one of his own romantic reveries?

"I don't like snow and ice very much," Kyna lied. "I like the world much better when it's warm."

They were nearing the long drive that led up to his house, but she felt as if they were driving through the gates of some formidable prison as he turned through the line of ice-coated trees that marked the beginnings of his property.

"I haven't had much warmth in my world lately." Blade didn't seem to be aware of how his words were affecting her as he slowed down for the last curve before the house, but then she saw he was very much aware of her nervousness and was intent on increasing it. "How about you, Kyna? Do those blueprints you love so much keep you warm at night?"

"If this is a business lunch, let's keep it business." Kyna pulled up the handle on her door before the car had completely rolled to a stop but was prevented from getting out by his hand on her arm.

"Hold on." He smiled, letting go of her as soon as he was certain they were no longer moving. "Wait for me to help you. The ground is slippery, and I don't want you to break either one of those long, beautiful legs of yours." His eyes swept up her body to her face. "I want us to enjoy every minute of our"—his gaze lingered on her breathlessly parted lips—"lunch."

11

~cccccccccc~

"Make yourself at home," Blade instructed politely, shrugging out of his overcoat after taking hers and hanging it up in the closet. As she stepped across the slate foyer, he strode past her into the living room, taking off his suit coat and throwing it over the back of the couch before heading for the kitchen. "I'm going to set us up out in the dining room so we can enjoy the view of the river during lunch. Why don't you pour yourself a glass of wine while I get things ready. You know where the bar is."

Glad he couldn't see her expression, Kyna walked to the built-in bar and found a glass. A bottle of Asti Spumante was chilling in the ice bucket, and her discomfort increased. Blade had evidently been quite certain she would join him for lunch. Why? Why had he coerced her into it? She didn't think she could face another scene with him, not without disclosing how easily he could hurt her.

"I made a Caesar's salad this morning," he called from the kitchen. "I get a craving for it when it gets cold outside; reminds me of the sunnier climate in southern Italy. Besides, I like to eat light at lunch. How about you? Will a large salad hold you until dinner?"

The one-sided rambling conversation didn't require Kyna's response until he posed the last question. If she didn't know better, Kyna would have thought Blade was suffering from an attack of nervousness.

"A salad would be fine," she called back, amazed that her voice didn't reveal the unsteady state of her own nerves. Sipping from her glass of wine, she walked slowly through the living room, avoiding looking over her shoulder at the suspended staircase that led upstairs to Blade's bedroom. She knew what the sight would do to her already overwound senses and quickened her pace as she escaped into the dining room.

Her thoughts were not as easy to avoid, but she managed it by standing in front of the glass doors that led to the snow-covered deck, devoting all of her attention to the view outside. Patches of ice and snow decorated the limestone cliffs overlooking the river. As Blade had said, the water was still moving, but it was icy at the snow-dusted edges. The trees, devoid of leaves, were coated with a thin layer of ice that refracted every colored ray of the sun, creating an illusion of a crystalline forest. A lone squirrel had forsaken its warm nest and hopped on the ground between two trees, digging until he'd uncovered an acorn, then scurrying away to enjoy his lunch in a more sheltered location.

Looking up, Kyna spotted a pair of cardinals perched on a low limb by the bird feeder Blade had placed just beyond the deck. The male was a vibrant red dash of color amidst the glistening backdrop of white snow and black branches as he stood sentry while his mate dropped gracefully to the feeder's perch. The smaller, less colorful female ate contentedly under the watchful protection of her mate; then the roles were reversed. Watching the cardinals, Kyna was reminded of the way so many of nature's creatures mated for life and shared equally in the duties of building a home, raising their young and protecting each other. That was the kind of relationship she wanted with a man, a natural give-and-take between equal partners.

She shifted her gaze from the cardinals, the thoughts they evoked making her uneasy. The stark beauty of the many miniature frozen waterfalls on the cliffs was a much safer view, and she concentrated on them. Sunlight danced across the icy formations, melting the edges so that drops of water fell on the lower rocks and eventually froze, creating a jagged effect. "You were right," Kyna declared. "The view from here is lovely."

Perhaps she could endure this time with Blade by keeping to safe subjects like the view and the weather. Maybe he'd decide she'd developed into a colossal bore, cut short their lunch and drive her right back to the city. She heard him step into the room behind her but didn't turn around. "I'm glad we have some snow for Christmas this year. It always puts me in a more festive mood."

Blade was setting the table but posed a question before returning to the kitchen for the salad and rolls. "What are your plans for the holidays?"

A sad expression came into Kyna's eyes. "I'll probably spend Christmas Day at my parents' home, but I can afford only a day away from the store. This is our busiest time."

If Blade noted her wistful expression, he didn't comment on it as he placed their food on the table. "I know what you mean. Mother always plans a big meal along with some other festivities, and I'm going over there for a while. I'll probably be back in the office the next day to clear a few year-end things up."

Kyna couldn't allow herself to think of how different Christmas could be if they were together. "You haven't put up any Christmas decorations. All this wood and stone would be a beautiful backdrop for greenery."

"Didn't seem much point since I'd be the only one to see them, and I'm not here much as it is." His explanation was given in an expressionless tone, but the words were filled with meaning as he held her gaze from across the room. She was aware too late that her comment about the lack of decorations had been a mistake.

Uncomfortable meeting the flat look in his eyes, Kyna started toward the table. "It looks delicious," she offered, wondering if they could possibly make enough small talk to endure their luncheon. She found herself weighing every comment to make sure it couldn't be applied in any way to their estrangement. Conversation was conducted in a stilted manner until they'd finished eating.

Blade drained his wineglass, then tossed his napkin on the table. Whatever unspoken truce there had been was broken, for now that the meal was apparently over, he went on the attack. "I assume the busy season is why I haven't heard from you."

"I didn't think you'd want to hear from me." Kyna sighed, seeing, by the stubborn thrust of Blade's chin, the vibrant color in his eyes and the firm set of his lips, that he wouldn't allow her to steer the conversation back to safe ground. Knowing there was no way she could avoid the confrontation, she decided the best defense was a good offense.

She matched his belligerent, sarcastic tone. "After all, weren't you hoping to find someone to marry before your stamina for affairs runs out? I didn't want to exhaust you and hurt some other woman's chances."

He displayed remarkable outward control, but Kyna could tell that her words had struck a nerve. Her green eyes were drawn to the slight pulse at his temple until he was aware that she had noted his reaction. Her lips twitched when he brushed his hand through his hair until it fell over, the telltale signal of his anger.

His next thrust was not verbal but visual. He caught her gaze, then melted the green shards of ice beneath her lashes with twin torches of burnished brown flames. "No woman has a chance with me until I can forget how your body feels against mine. How your eyes beckon to me when we're making love. How your lips part for my kisses."

"Blade," she warned, unsuccessfully attempting to forestall the sensual warmth that was rapidly spreading inside her. "Our affair is over. You broke off with me, not the other way around." Deliberately, she lowered her head until her features were hidden behind the dark waves of her hair, then began toying with her empty wineglass. "I'd like another glass of wine, please."

"Of course." He scraped his chair back and crossed the room to lift the bottle of wine from the bucket resting on the credenza.

She thought the request would break the mood, but when he returned to the table, he didn't return to his seat; he came up behind her. Although he didn't touch her, one hand grasped the back of her chair.

"Here you are." He held out the glass to the side, slightly above her shoulder. In order for her to take it, she had to swivel in her seat, and he had positioned his hand on her chair so her breast would brush against his fingers if she turned.

She completed the maneuver as swiftly as possible, not hiding her furious expression, which was met with a knowing grin. She felt like throwing the wine in his face but sensed he was just waiting for her to lose her temper so he'd be justified in taking action. She could almost feel his will working its way inside her. He wanted her, wanted her back in his arms where he felt she belonged. She wanted it, too, with all of her being, but they couldn't go back to the way they had been. Their needs were too different. "Why are you doing this, Blade?" she said chokingly, aware of every breath he drew as he lingered behind her.

His hands closed over her shoulders, stroking the soft material of her dress down her arms and back up again. "I want you, Kyna." The hoarse whisper fanned the exposed skin at the side of her neck and sent shivers of reaction racing down her spine. "I've never wanted any woman as badly."

He reached for her hand and drew her up from the chair. "I can't forget you." His fingers tightened on hers as he pulled her into his arms. His mouth sought hers, lips hungrily seeking the taste he had done without for far too long.

Kyna knew she shouldn't have let it happen, but she was as eager to be back in his arms as he was to have her. She trembled with rising passion as his tongue delved into her mouth. His compelling attack located her every weakness, an overwhelming onslaught consisting of his kisses, the expert stroking of his hands, the hard thrust of his body against her pliant softness. Before she could pull back to regroup her defenses, she was overcome by his tactics and fully engaged in the sensual skirmish that escalated swiftly into a passionate campaign fought on all fronts.

Impatiently, he pulled the gold combs from her hair, then sank his hands into the shiny black length. He buried his face in it, breathing deeply. "I've been captured in this web," he whispered. "Remembering the smell of your hair, the feel of it cascading over me like a million separate strands of silk, has been driving me mad."

Yielding to her own temptation, Kyna lifted her hand to his face, tracing each handsome feature, then kissed him, her tongue probing his mouth. She was as greedy for him after their imposed famine as he was for her. Her feverish whispers joined his. "I've missed you, Blade. So much . . . so much."

It was as if they were melting into one another, giving and taking all they had missed during their time apart. There was no protest when Blade guided them out of the dining room toward the stairs, no hesitation when they mounted them side by side, hand in hand.

Facing each other, they began to undress, savoring the sight of one another as their clothes slowly fell to the floor. Kyna sensed they were equal partners in an intoxicating sensual interplay, the first in a series of primitive rituals that would eventually lead to nature's ancient rites of passion. She could feel her heart beating, pulsating like a native drum. She was vibrating, trembling with desire for him as he approached her. He came slowly, a golden giant of a man seeking harmony with his feminine counterpart. Their eyes met, dark with longing, soft with tumultuous emotion.

When he stopped in front of her, he didn't touch her but caressed every inch of her soft skin with his eyes, worshiped the exotic loveliness of her face, adored the shimmering black veil of her hair. He opened his arms, and she walked into them, burning up with sensation. His skin felt hot, textured and throbbing beneath her fingertips. She laid her cheek against the gleaming pectoral muscles of his chest, breathing in his male scent. "Love me, Blade," she demanded, her voice breathless with longing.

"Kyna," he murmured thickly, scooping her up in his arms. He carried her to the bed, lowered her tenderly to the mattress, then came down on top of her. There was so much hunger in both of them that there was no place for light caresses, no time for soft words of challenge or encouragement. They both knew what they wanted and took it.

Inflamed by the heated crush of his body, Kyna's movements became frantic. Blade claimed her mouth, grasping her hair to hold her head in place while his tongue drove deeply. Her feverish moans increased his appetite for her, and he shuddered with need as her soft palms stroked over his shoulders, her long fingers digging into his skin.

He parted her thighs with his own, groaning as she accommodated every move he made with the wild female motions he remembered so well. Unable to hold back his frenzied need for her, he entered her swiftly, holding his breath as she answered his challenge, arching herself to meet him. Entwined in exotic harmony, they moved as one, spiraling higher and higher, then mindlessly swirling up and beyond any height they had ever reached.

Kyna's first sensation as she returned to an awareness of her surroundings was the feel of Blade's head resting between her breasts, his damp blond hair brushed by the agitated motion of her breathing. He was as breathless as she, his weight pressing her down on the sheets, his fingers still trapped in her hair. "God, I needed you," he said haltingly.

How she loved him. Nothing mattered but him, being with him, needing him and being needed. She began stroking his head, tenderly brushing the gold strands away from the warm skin at his temples. "Oh, Blade, I never want to lose you again."

"You won't," he reassured, the burnished fire of passion still glowing in his eyes as he slid across her, turning over on his back as he drew her up alongside him, placing her head on his shoulder. "You've won, Kyna. We're going to do things your way. My ego was doing all the talking the night I walked out on you, but since then I've learned I'd rather have you in my bed than sleep alone with my pride. Marriage is out for us, but I still want you so badly, I'll accept any other terms."

"Terms?" Kyna asked, confused. She had thought they had finally reached an understanding, both acknowledging that they weren't whole without the other. Didn't that mean marriage to him? Did he no longer want her as a wife? She reached for the sheet and pulled it over her nakedness, averting her face so he wouldn't see the anxiety in her eyes.

"You don't want any commitment," Blade said. "And I've realized that's probably best for me, too. I know what kind of work it takes to make a go of any business, and neither of us has the time to give to a marriage. I'll be taking over as president the first of the year, and your new store will be open for business in March. We'll both have to devote most of our time to our careers, but we can see each other whenever we can."

"Whenever we can," Kyna repeated dumbly, feeling as if she were being beaten by every word he spoke.

"I still think you should move in here. That way

you'd be more available for these kind of sessions in bed."

It seemed he had their future planned out, but Kyna was having a difficult time following his logic. Didn't their lovemaking mean any more to him than that? Was his only concern with logistics, making certain they would find adequate time for these kind of "sessions"? Was today an example of what their future held? Stolen snatches of time in the middle of the day?

When she didn't respond, he continued quickly. "If you're concerned that I'd try to smother you, don't be. I learned my lesson. You and I will both be free to make our own decisions. You won't have to answer to me or I to you? Fair?"

She withdrew from the warm strength of his arms, keeping her face averted from his as she moved off the bed so he wouldn't see the shimmer of tears she couldn't control. "What's wrong?" he asked in a puzzled tone.

She remained silent as she picked up her scattered clothing, aware without looking that his eyes were following her every movement. The words she'd hurled at him in anger haunted her, and she knew he expected her to agree with this latest proposal, so different from the one he'd offered that night at her apartment. Could she blame him? Could she possibly expect a man as proud as Blade to humble himself and propose marriage again after she'd made it clear she wanted no commitment at that point in her life?

She needed time, time to gather her shattered emotions together and form an answer, but he didn't give her that time. "Kyna?" He demanded her attention, and she turned back, catching her breath at the sight of his magnificent naked body rising from the bed.

She didn't quite know how to answer him when every part of her was screaming to declare her love for him and beg him to reconsider, to forgive the words she'd thrown at him before, understand that they weren't what she'd felt. Her fear that any explanations of that night were too late prompted her to make a show of carefully draping her dress over her arm, needing to stall even for a few seconds longer until her tear-choked throat would allow speech. At last, she mumbled, "I don't think moving in with you is a good idea. As you said, we both want our independence, and I doubt we'd have that if we lived together." She whirled and escaped into the bathroom, locking the door between them before the tears spilled over onto her cheeks.

Didn't he realize how degrading his proposition was? Having her near him for convenience, nothing more? How long would he want her? He'd said he couldn't forget her—yet. If he'd only said he'd never forget her, that there would never be another woman in his life, she would agree to live with him, commit herself to sharing their lives. Sharing and equality were never mentioned, and she knew that no matter how much she yearned to spend every night in his arms, she couldn't agree to the terms he was now offering.

She wrapped a towel around her hair and stepped into the shower. The noise of the cascading water concealed the sobs that escaped from her shuddering body, the warm water failing to dispel the cold that permeated her entire being. Knowing she couldn't remain in the shower much longer, she gained control of herself, turned off the taps and stepped out of the steamy chamber. She dressed slowly, then used one of Blade's brushes lying on the lavatory counter to smooth the tangles in her hair before stepping back into the bedroom, not sure what she was going to say to Blade but knowing she had to say something. Nothing had been settled between them.

She had expected to find him waiting for her and was surprised to find the room empty. There was no sign of him; his clothing had been picked up, and he was gone. Assuming he'd dressed and was somewhere on the first floor, she started for the stairs, faltering in her step when she heard the sound of another shower at the opposite end of the hallway. Relieved that she had a few more moments to herself, Kyna made her way down the winding stairs on shaking legs, keeping a tight grip on the metal rail.

For a fleeting moment, she considered calling a taxi and leaving while Blade was still upstairs but realized that his home was located far enough away from the city that it would probably take a taxi too long to arrive. Blade would easily be out of the shower and dressed before she could effect such a cowardly retreat. If only she'd suggested she follow him in her car, but he'd whisked her out of the office and was well on his way to his home before she'd realized what he was about.

You're a big girl, Kyna O'Brien, she reminded herself. You got yourself into this mess, and you'll just have to get yourself out. You think you can handle yourself in any situation, so you're just going to have to prove it. She continued to lecture herself while she listened uneasily to Blade's movements above her.

Settling herself on the couch, she tried leafing through a magazine she found lying on the end table but had no idea what any of the articles were about as her brain raced to find a way to talk with Blade, to be able to turn down his suggestion without losing what little self-esteem he'd left her. She'd have to be as coolly objective as he had been when he proposed she move in with him. She'd rejected several ineffective possibilities by the time Blade came downstairs.

"I'll get your coat," he said, going straight to the foyer closet. "I believe you said you had several things planned for the afternoon, and I wouldn't want to ruin your busy schedule."

Was that all? Surely he'd expect some elaboration on her refusal to move in with him. Wasn't he going to try to argue her out of that decision? He couldn't be giving up that easily . . . unless he really didn't care. Maybe that afternoon had been enough, at least for a while.

Uneasily, Kyna crossed the living room to the foyer and silently slipped into her coat as Blade held it for her. Was it wishful imagination that his hands lingered briefly on her shoulders and that he remained so close behind her that she could feel his breath lifting a few strands of her hair?

He stepped away from her, and Kyna opened her eyes, suddenly realizing she'd closed them and would have leaned back into his arms if he hadn't stepped back. She stood where she was until she heard him slide his arms into his own heavy coat and his hand turn the knob of the door. Casting another look through the living-room windows, hoping to gain some serenity from the peaceful view, Kyna turned and followed Blade out the door.

He said nothing as he took her elbow in a firm grasp and safely guided her down the steps and across the glistening walkway. She lost her footing once and would have fallen if Blade hadn't quickly grabbed her around the waist with both arms. Her hands automatically spread across his chest, and her face involuntarily turned up toward his. "Thank you, Blade."

"We all need to depend on someone sometimes, even you." He released her and turned her toward the car again. No further words were exchanged between them as Blade drove back to the city, and Kyna held herself stiffly in the seat beside him, knowing, though they were separated by mere inches in the confines of the car, there were too many misunderstandings between them to shorten the light-years of distance that separated their feelings.

He wheeled into the parking lot of Palmer & Young and stopped his car a few feet from hers but didn't turn off the engine. Assuming he meant for her to get out and allow him to drive on to his reserved parking place without further conversation, Kyna reached for the door handle. "Not yet, Kyna." His leather-gloved hand fell to her shoulder and forced her to turn toward him. "I have a few more things I'd like to say to you."

"Blade, I don't think there's any more to be said between us. I won't move in with you. I—"

"I don't understand you. I've tried to do things your way, but that didn't work out, either. Do you even know what you want? I don't think I ever found out who you really are! I thought all this time that I could get around all that talk about independence and your drive for success, that it was only a protective façade gilding the vibrant, warm woman beneath. There isn't anything underneath, is there? Just like a cheap imitation; if you scratch the surface, you discover nothing but cold lead."

"That's not true. I'm not—"

He didn't listen to her denial but rambled on as if he were purging himself of a long-imprisoned wrath. "God help me, but I still want you even if I can only have the surface." He reached into his pocket, extracted a small, flat package and tossed it into her lap.

"I waited weeks, hoping you'd come to me, until I finally couldn't stand it any longer, and I'd hoped today would make you change your mind about us. I won't do it again. If there's a next time, you'll have to come to me of your own free will. I won't coerce you into a showdown again." He hauled her across the seat and against him, lowering his mouth to hers, crushing her lips beneath his in a soul-rending possession. He kissed her as if it were his last chance to drink the essence of her, but every thrust of his tongue was a tormented promise of all she would be losing if she never saw him again, and then his lips were gone, and he was reaching across to open the door beside her.

12

~~~~~~~~~~~~~~~~~~~

Kyna muddled through the remaining days until Christmas Eve in a dazed stupor. Her actions were mechanical as she performed the many tasks necessary at the Gilded Lily during the day. She worked long after the boutique was closed each night, telling Lenore that she was completing the bookwork necessary at the end of each month. She knew her friend suspected there was another reason for the late hours Kyna was putting in but was thankful that once again the effervescent blonde didn't pry.

As long as she could concentrate on work, Kyna was able to keep thoughts of Blade out of the forefront, but the minute she stepped into her apartment each night, she was flooded with anguish. The tiny box he'd given her contained a gilded key, and Kyna knew without a doubt that it was a key to his house. She hadn't been able to touch the key, and it remained undisturbed on its bed of white satin, hidden from her view in the bottom of a dresser drawer.

Christmas Eve arrived, and Kyna packed an overnight case and a shopping bag of presents for her family into her Volkswagen and headed the little car north. She avoided taking a route that would be anywhere near the river, not wanting to see any reminder of Blade and his home no matter how many miles she might be from it. She was devoid of tears, having cried herself to sleep every night in the loneliness of her apartment.

As she left the rolling river valley in the middle of the state, she concentrated on the visit ahead of her. Christmas was a time to share with those whom you loved, and no matter how estranged she had been from her parents, this was a time to put it aside and allow the promise of the season of brotherly love to take over. She thought about all the traditions her family observed each holiday and the various relatives who would gather at the O'Brien home the next day. She'd been an only child, but the O'Brien family was large, and the house would be overflowing with aunts, uncles and cousins on Christmas day, a rollicking gang of Irishmen celebrating their holiday together.

Since breaking off with Blade, she felt more alone than she ever had before and knew that she needed to bridge the gaping chasm that had spread between her parents and herself. What better time than Christmas? Barely two hours after she'd left Columbus, Kyna turned into the familiar driveway of her family home. Smoke was curling from the chimney, and as she opened the car door, she smelled the fragrance of the hardwood logs she knew were burning in the large brick fireplace in the living room. Extracting her things from the car, she started toward the house just as the front door flew open.

"Kyna, darlin'," her mother shouted from the porch. Kyna was in the gray-haired woman's arms and held close, her overnight case and packages scattered on the wooden porch floor. She was home, and for the first time in years, it felt good to be there.

"Merry Christmas, mama," she managed, and looked over her mother's shoulder to see her father standing in the doorway. There was a hesitant look on his face, and Kyna knew the first overture must come from her.

Tom O'Brien stood straight and tall, his green eyes misted as he savored the image of his daughter. Kyna's mother stepped away from her and busied herself scooping up her daughter's packages, knowing that this moment was between her husband and Kyna. They were two stubborn Irishmen who shared unyielding pride as well as the height, green eyes and straight black hair that proclaimed their relationship.

"Daddy?" Kyna took a step toward him, and then he held open his arms, and Kyna went willingly into them, not caring that they had last parted so angrily. She needed the succor of her parents' love.

"Merry Christmas, Kyna," Tom O'Brien huskily greeted her, then set her slightly away from him but kept one arm around her waist. "Can't stay out here much longer or we'll freeze to death and your mother won't have anyone to eat the fine dinner she's prepared." Giving her a twinkling wink, he pulled her into the house and closed the door behind them.

Breathing in the familiar holiday scents of the house, Kyna grinned as she pulled off her coat and gloves. "Smells like she's made all the usual spread." She giggled when she saw the trays of cookies and other treats already arranged on the large, old-fashioned sideboard in the dining room. "She must be expecting the entire clan tomorrow."

"You know your mother," her father confirmed. "Grab a few cookies and come on into the living room with me. There's a good fire, and it'll warm you up." He started past her, then teased, "You ever get that heater to work in that little car of yours?"

"Keeps the worst of the cold out," Kyna admitted before sinking her teeth into a date-filled bar, one of her mother's many specialties. She folded her long legs beneath her and sat down on the hooked rug in front of the raised hearth. A tray containing an ironstone chocolate pot and several mugs sat on the hearth close enough to the protective screen to keep the contents of the hand-painted blue and white pot warm. Kyna knew without asking that it contained hot chocolate and poured herself a cup; and after receiving a nod from her father, she poured one for him.

She reached for one of the large pillows stacked nearby and tucked it behind her back as she leaned against the bricks and sipped the steaming chocolate. The mug nearly slipped from her grasp when her father asked, "How's your business going, Kyna? I imagine December's been a big month for you and Lenore." She braced herself for any remarks that might reflect the lack of confidence he'd always had for the success of her venture, but when none came, she looked up.

He was leaning forward, cradling his mug between his large hands, staring at the flickering flames that licked along the logs in the grate. His words had been delivered in a sincere tone, and Kyna gathered courage, sensing that her father's attitude might have changed. She began to explain how well the boutique had been doing; then, with more confidence, she launched into the plans she and Lenore had for the future, describing the new location and the reasons for the move.

"Sounds like you two girls have built up quite a sound business. I'm glad for you, Kyna." He smiled his infectious Irish smile and, when Kyna returned it, continued. "I—ah—I think I owe you an apology."

Knowing how much a statement like that was costing his pride, and grateful for what he'd already said, Kyna tried to stop him. "It's all right, daddy."

"No, honey, let me finish. Four years is too long a time for a father and his daughter to carry a grudge, and we need to lay all our cards on the table. I was wrong, and I admit it. You've done well, and I'm proud of you."

"Oh, dad, thank you. That means so much to me."

"I've always been proud of you, honey. First because you were the prettiest little baby girl I ever saw and then because you were so smart in school. As mad as I was, I was even proud of you for sticking up for yourself and believing in yourself enough to go after what you really wanted."

Kyna closed the space between them and threw her arms around her father's neck, the tears of joy coursing down her cheeks mingled with those on her father's. "I needed this, dad."

"So did I, so did I." He patted her hair and held her close. "I suppose I wasn't ready to let you grow up, and I wanted to protect you from any hurt or disappointment for as long as I could. I love you, Kyna; don't ever doubt that. The hardest thing anyone can do is let go of their child and let them make their own way.

"Your mother and I waited a long time for the miracle of having you. You were the only one God blessed us with, and we were too afraid sometimes that we'd lose you. I always wanted to keep you safe. Maybe we were a little selfish in hoping we could always have you close by. I never wanted to let you go, but I pushed you away."

"I'm back now, dad." Kyna straightened and wiped away her tears with the back of her hand. She managed a crooked little smile. "Columbus isn't so very far away, you know. Maybe now we can manage to see each other more often than we have."

"I'd like that, honey."

"Will you come to the grand opening of the new shop? We're going to open just before St. Patrick's Day, and there'll be a big celebration at the mall. You and mama could stay over, and we could all go enjoy the parade."

"Remember when we did that once when you were a little girl?"

She was back, really back. The prodigal daughter returned and welcomed into the loving folds of her family. She laughed through most of dinner as her parents brought her up-to-date with the other members of the family, who would be arriving the next day. After dinner, they walked the short distance to the little church where she'd worshiped most of her life and once again shared the beauty of the Christmas Eve candlelight service with her parents.

That night, as she lay in the narrow sleigh bed in her childhood room, Kyna's mind drifted through memories, but it was not the ghosts of Christmas past or Christmas future that haunted her. Blade. Always Blade. His smiles were replaced by the cold, flat expression he'd had when she'd seen him last. The feel of his lips soft and tender against hers would evaporate, and his mouth would become brutal against hers.

Her father thought she was a success, but the joy she should be experiencing in his approval was tarnished. She wasn't a success, not really. Her business was doing well and by all projections would continue to grow, but it was a hollow victory. Like Dickens's Scrooge, her race for success had robbed her of something far more precious than gold. While she might accrue a healthy bank account, as well as recognition in the commercial community, those rewards weren't of any more real value than the gilded medals awarded the winner of a marathon. Beneath the surface, they were as cold and worthless as Blade had labeled her.

"I was even proud that you believed enough in yourself to go after what you wanted." Kyna sat up in the bed. She knew how she felt about Blade and knew what she had to do to prove herself to him. She replayed their last meeting. Had he really meant what he'd implied in his suggested living arrangement? Could his accusations when they'd parted come from hurt? If they did, there was a chance for them, and she knew she had to try to win his love. Like an Olympic runner, she'd go for the gold—a golden-haired man she couldn't afford to lose. If he rejected the love she would offer him, then so be it; she'd find a way to live without him. But if he didn't . . . It was a chance she had to take.

Lying back in the bed, Kyna formed a plan in her mind. It had to work; it just had to. She fell asleep without tears streaming down her cheeks for the first time in days. A slight smile softened her face as her dreams spun images of a tall man in jogging shorts, first on a leaf-strewn path and then waiting at the end of a finish line with a golden key dangling from a ribbon in his hand.

Early the next morning, Kyna was on her way back to Columbus. Her parents hadn't offered any protest to her abrupt leaving after she'd told them about Blade. "I knew something was wrong," her mother had said. "Your eyes just weren't as sparkling as they should be."

It had been her father's words that served to keep her from wavering. "You set your mind to building a business and did it. Sometimes it's good to be a stiff-necked Irishman, and this is one of those times. Get going . . . but drive carefully, honey. We don't want to lose you."

There was little traffic during the two-hour return trip, and Kyna surmised that most people were already with their loved ones. By the end of the day, she hoped she would be, too. Her confidence that her decision was right never wavered as she made her first stop of the day at her own apartment, then the Gilded Lily, then Blade's house.

It was about noon by the time she used the golden key he'd given her to let herself into his house. After several trips back to her car, she'd emptied it of all its contents, and a small mountain of sundry packages was heaped in the foyer. After hanging up her coat, she pushed up her sleeves and went to work.

Knowing Blade was enjoying a grand feast with Barbara and Paul, and guessing that she had all day and possibly most of the evening, Kyna flipped on the radio, tuned in a station that carried nothing but Christmas carols and started hanging the garlands she'd ripped off the walls at the boutique. She'd rummaged in his garage and basement until she found a small folding ladder, and within the first hour, the large limestone fireplace wall had been transformed. It took but a few more minutes to set up the small artificial tree and replace the golden lilies that had decorated it for the past month in the display window at the store.

She was satisfied that she'd done as much as she could with the living room but wished she'd had ornaments other than all the gilded artificial flowers, the very symbols of her mistakes. Sighing, she gathered up the packing paper and carried the boxes to the basement. Remembering that her car was still parked near the front door, she slipped her jacket back on and raced outside to move it inside the garage. She wanted to surprise him completely and hoped that he'd leave his car outside when he returned.

Those chores done, she went to work in the kitchen. Her mother had easily supplied everything she needed, and Kyna found plenty of trays and serving dishes in Blade's cupboards to arrange all the food her mother had packed for her. The microwave oven, installed above the range top, would come in handy later on when, within minutes, she would be able to serve up a dinner as delicious as that being eaten by her family at that very moment. Checking the wines in the rack built into one wall of the kitchen, Kyna selected a Brut champagne and tucked it in a bucket of ice.

Glancing at her watch, she was surprised to see that most of the afternoon was gone but guessed she'd still have time to complete the final stages of her plan. All that was left was relieving the foyer of her own luggage and then preparing herself for the meeting with Blade. Hanging in the hall closet was the garment bag containing the floor-length green velvet gown she'd whisked off a rack at the Gilded Lily during her rampage through the store that morning. Lenore had urged her for a month to take the dress for her own, saying the color and simple, classic design were perfect for her, but Kyna had refused, saying she wouldn't have the right occasion to wear it. But now she did.

The long-sleeved, deep V-necked gown connoted an evening at home, lounging by a crackling fire. . . . Fire! She'd have to set some logs in the fireplace and get a fire going before she started getting herself ready. She sped back to the living room, hoping to find a supply of logs in the large brass coal bucket that stood beside the fireplace, but was dismayed to find it empty.

Pulling on her jacket once again, she raced outside, praying that Blade had a supply of firewood somewhere, and she wouldn't have to forage for dead wood in the surrounding forest. Almost giving up as she raced through the garage and around it, she spied a small shed at the back of the garage and anxiously pulled open the door. It was filled with carefully stacked dry wood, and Kyna ran back and forth several times until she was satisfied that there was plenty of fuel for the fireplace.

After arranging a bed of kindling and then a stack of heavier logs, Kyna knelt on the hearth and tried to get a fire started. Each time she managed to get a small flickering flame started among the kindling and paper, it would die out almost as soon as it started. After several attempts, all she had to show for her efforts was some charred paper and a lot of smoke. She leaned back on her heels in total disgust. Feeling completely exasperated, she decided to give it one more try before giving up.

Engrossed in keeping the faltering flame going and puffing at the small success her final attempt was achieving, she didn't hear the sound of a key in the door. Her first indication that she was no longer alone was the sound of Blade's voice. "What the—Kyna?"

She turned sharply to the sound, blushing. "Ah . . . Blade. I didn't expect you so soon." Rising slowly to her feet, her embarrassment grew as she looked down at her soiled, rumpled jeans and the smudges on her tattered sweatshirt. "What are you doing here?"

"I live here." He advanced farther into the room,

unbuttoning his overcoat and removing his gloves. He tossed them on the couch and started toward her, then stopped as his eyes took in all the decorations she'd provided. "What are you doing here?"

Now that the moment was at hand, Kyna could think of nothing to say. The carefully rehearsed lines she'd composed were supposed to be delivered by a beautifully groomed woman lounging casually on the couch in a dark green velvet gown. They didn't seem appropriate in her present attire. She studied her grimy hands and chanced a glance at Blade, wishing he'd say something, not just stand a few feet away, staring at her. Remembering her father's words, she lifted her chin and stared back at him. Believe in yourself, Kyna O'Brien. Go after what you want. You're not in costume, nor is the stage completely set. Improvise.

"I'm making the first move; that's what I'm doing." She drank in every detail of him with her eyes wide, from the top of his gold-streaked head and the handsome lines of his face to his broad shoulders beneath the deep red sweater he wore above charcoal flannel slacks that swathed the long, hard muscles of his hips and thighs. She wanted him to open his arms to her, make it easy to have this reunion, but he stood mercilessly implacable. Damn it, do something, Blade, Kyna pleaded inwardly. Help me.

Kyna couldn't stand the silence that stretched between them any longer and erupted in anger. "You weren't supposed to be back yet. This isn't the way I planned it. I'm not ready. I couldn't get the fire started, and I'm still in my old dirty jeans, and I'm a complete mess, and I wanted to be all dressed in a velvet gown, showered and smelling good. I—"

"You're a beautiful mess." He interrupted her semihysterical tirade, crossed the space between them and wrapped her in his arms. His lips found hers in a bittersweet kiss, filled with longing and promise. Kyna's arms wound around his neck, and she clung to his strong body, giving all she could as she returned his kiss, her tongue enticingly winding around his as she feasted on the bounty of being in his arms.

"Oh, Blade, I love you so much." She rested her palms on each side of his face and placed small kisses across his chin and jaw and returned to his mouth. "I do need you," she murmured against his lips, and their mouths elicited fiery responses in each other as he gathered her closer.

"Kyna, Kyna, are you going to include me in every day of your life?"

"If you'll let me."

"If I'll let you?" He loosened his hold on her but kept her within the circle of his arms as he stared down at her. "What do you think I've been trying to do ever since we met. I love you, Kyna O'Brien. I want you. I want to protect you. I want to help you when you'll let me. I—" He stopped and gave her a quizzical look. "Will you help me? Will you be my partner in life?"

Her body filled with joy. A partner in his life. "That's exactly what I want."

He buried his face in her hair, breathing deeply. "Mmm, I love the smell of your hair—a bit smoky, perhaps, but it still smells good." He raised his head and planted a quick kiss on her forehead, then began to laugh, the sound rumbling from his chest and vibrating against her. Her eyes widened in confusion, but she didn't have to wait long for an explanation. His thumb brushed across her nose. "Allow me, my love. You have soot all over your face. Why don't you go get cleaned up and into that velvet dress you planned to seduce me with. I'll get a fire started."

He released her and bent toward the fireplace,

reached in and pulled a chain dangling inside. "Looks to me as if I got home just in time. You didn't have the damper open. If you were any better at starting fires, the house would be filled with even more smoke." He added to the chagrin she was feeling over her inept attempts at fire making by placing a single match at the base of the grate and turning a small brass knob at the corner of the fireplace. The flames ignited, and the wood was crackling within seconds.

"How did you do that?"

He grinned over his shoulder as he dusted his hands, then slowly stood up. "There's a gas jet—starts a fire every time." He gave her a push toward the stairs. "Get going or I'll join you up there and you'll never get the chance to put on that dress you were raving about." He looked down at his watch, frowning as the second hand swept around the numbers. "Now! You have ten minutes."

Kyna's feet flew toward the staircase and had mounted three of them before she remembered that her dress was still hanging in the closet. Careening through the living room and back again, she took the carpeted stairs as fast as she could and dashed toward Blade's bedroom. The fastest shower ever recorded in her lifetime followed, and barely dry, she slipped into lacy undergarments and the velvet gown. Rummaging through her overnight case, which she'd managed to grab in her flight up the stairs, she found her brush and cosmetic bag. She used her remaining time to brush her hair vigorously and apply a minimum of makeup and a quick spray of her favorite perfume. In her haste in packing, she'd forgotten to include appropriate shoes, but the golden slippers her mother had given her for Christmas seemed perfect. Calming herself by taking deep breaths, she walked slowly to the stairs, determined to make her grand entrance, even if it was anticlimactic and her feet were sheathed in house slippers.

True to his threat, Blade was about to come up after her. His hand rested on the rail, and one foot was on the bottom step. He stepped back as she began to descend, and Kyna knew by the glow in his beautiful eyes that her efforts wouldn't go unrewarded. She'd won the race for the gold, and her award, a lifetime of love, was waiting for her at the bottom of the stairs.

YOU'LL BE SWEPT AWAY WITH SILHOUETTE DESIRE

$1.75 each

1 ☐ James	5 ☐ Baker	8 ☐ Dee
2 ☐ Monet	6 ☐ Mallory	9 ☐ Simms
3 ☐ Clay	7 ☐ St. Claire	10 ☐ Smith
4 ☐ Carey		

$1.95 each

11 ☐ James	29 ☐ Michelle	47 ☐ Michelle	65 ☐ Allison
12 ☐ Palmer	30 ☐ Lind	48 ☐ Powers	66 ☐ Langtry
13 ☐ Wallace	31 ☐ James	49 ☐ James	67 ☐ James
14 ☐ Valley	32 ☐ Clay	50 ☐ Palmer	68 ☐ Browning
15 ☐ Vernon	33 ☐ Powers	51 ☐ Lind	69 ☐ Carey
16 ☐ Major	34 ☐ Milan	52 ☐ Morgan	70 ☐ Victor
17 ☐ Simms	35 ☐ Major	53 ☐ Joyce	71 ☐ Joyce
18 ☐ Ross	36 ☐ Summers	54 ☐ Fulford	72 ☐ Hart
19 ☐ James	37 ☐ James	55 ☐ James	73 ☐ St. Clair
20 ☐ Allison	38 ☐ Douglass	56 ☐ Douglass	74 ☐ Douglass
21 ☐ Baker	39 ☐ Monet	57 ☐ Michelle	75 ☐ McKenna
22 ☐ Durant	40 ☐ Mallory	58 ☐ Mallory	76 ☐ Michelle
23 ☐ Sunshine	41 ☐ St. Claire	59 ☐ Powers	77 ☐ Lowell
24 ☐ Baxter	42 ☐ Stewart	60 ☐ Dennis	78 ☐ Barber
25 ☐ James	43 ☐ Simms	61 ☐ Simms	79 ☐ Simms
26 ☑ Palmer	44 ☐ West	62 ☐ Monet	80 ☐ Palmer
27 ☐ Conrad	45 ☐ Clay	63 ☐ Dee	81 ☐ Kennedy
28 ☐ Lovan	46 ☐ Chance	64 ☐ Milan	82 ☐ Clay

YOU'LL BE SWEPT AWAY WITH SILHOUETTE DESIRE

$1.95 each

83 ☐ Chance	99 ☐ Major	115 ☐ James	131 ☐ Larson
84 ☐ Powers	100 ☐ Howard	116 ☐ Joyce	132 ☐ McCoy
85 ☐ James	101 ☐ Morgan	117 ☐ Powers	133 ☐ Monet
86 ☐ Malek	102 ☐ Palmer	118 ☐ Milan	134 ☐ McKenna
87 ☐ Michelle	103 ☐ James	119 ☐ John	135 ☐ Charlton
88 ☐ Trevor	104 ☐ Chase	120 ☐ Clay	136 ☐ Martel
89 ☐ Ross	105 ☐ Blair	121 ☐ Browning	137 ☐ Ross
90 ☐ Roszel	106 ☐ Michelle	122 ☐ Trent	138 ☐ Chase
91 ☐ Browning	107 ☐ Chance	123 ☐ Paige	139 ☐ St. Claire
92 ☐ Carey	108 ☐ Gladstone	124 ☐ St. George	140 ☐ Joyce
93 ☐ Berk	109 ☐ Simms	125 ☐ Caimi	141 ☐ Morgan
94 ☐ Robbins	110 ☐ Palmer	126 ☐ Carey	142 ☐ Nicole
95 ☐ Summers	111 ☐ Browning	127 ☐ James	143 ☐ Allison
96 ☐ Milan	112 ☐ Nicole	128 ☐ Michelle	144 ☐ Evans
97 ☐ James	113 ☐ Cresswell	129 ☐ Bishop	
98 ☐ Joyce	114 ☐ Ross	130 ☐ Blair	

SILHOUETTE DESIRE, Department SD/6
1230 Avenue of the Americas
New York, NY 10020

Please send me the books I have checked above. I am enclosing $_____
(please add 75¢ to cover postage and handling. NYS and NYC residents please
add appropriate sales tax). Send check or money order—no cash or C.O.D.'s
please. Allow six weeks for delivery.

NAME _____

ADDRESS_____

CITY_____ STATE/ZIP_____

Silhouette Desire

Coming Next Month

Night Of The Magician by Stephanie James

Ariana knew that magician Lucian Hawk was the perfect choice to help her unmask a charlatan psychic, but she soon discovered that Lucian's most dangerous spell would be the passion she found in his arms.

Eternal Flame by Alicia Knight

The last thing Randy expected to find when she arrived home was a charming English journalist in her bathtub! Grant had no place else to stay during the Los Angeles Olympics, but did Randy's hospitality include giving her heart?

Territorial Rights by Melissa Scott

Meredith was horrified when fellow teacher Doug Traxler dared her to hike with his ecology class. But she accepted the challenge to find that Doug would open not only her mind but her heart.

In A Stranger's Arms by Nora Powers

As a woman in the macho world of rodeo Emily didn't believe she could combine her profession with love—until writer Alex Calloway. Suddenly, Emily was determined to lasso both her man and her career no matter what it took!

Double Game by Serena Galt

Carrie had thought of tennis superstar Nikolai Zanov as just another playboy—but when they played together at Wimbledon she discovered a tender and loving man. Who was the real Nikolai and what were the secrets that held them apart?

Dream Within A Dream by Suzanne Simms

Callie Foster had worked hard to create a secure life for herself and she wasn't going to shake it up for any man—especially ruthless Reid Dillon. Callie fought the memory of their passion but after Reid's possession she would never be the same.